P9-CCW-896

A Hidden Magic

A HIDDEN MAGIC

·by Vivian Vande Velde ·

illustrated by Trina Schart Hyman

Crown Publishers, Inc. · NEW YORK

Published by Crown Publishers, Inc., One Park Avenue, New York, New York 10016
and simultaneously in Canada by General Publishing Company Limited

Manufactured in the United States of America

CROWN is a trademark of Crown Publishers, Inc.

Library of Congress Cataloging in Publication Data

Vande Velde, Vivian.
A hidden magic.

Summary: Lost in a magic forest and separated from
her prince, Princess Jennifer seeks help from a
kindly young sorcerer in battling an evil witch.
[1. Fantasy] I. Hyman, Trina Schart, ill. II. Title.
PZ7.V2773Hi 1985 [Fic] 85-16643
ISBN 0-517-55534-4

Typography by Jane Byers Bierhorst
10 9 8 7 6 5 4 3 2 1
First Edition

FOR JIM—
prince, sorcerer, and husband

Contents

A Hidden Magic

Jennifer

Once upon a time—before kings and queens were replaced by an act of Congress and when kissing a frog still sometimes resulted in more than a case of warts—there lived a young princess named Jennifer.

Now Jennifer was not your average beautiful princess living in a magnificent palace. In fact, she was actually rather plain and shy, with the chubby, good-natured kind of face parents tend to call nice. And as for the magnificent palace—the kingdom over which Jennifer's father reigned was very tiny, and the nicest thing that could be said about the old castle was that it hadn't fallen down on anyone yet.

One morning in early spring Jennifer was lying on a sun-warmed rock by the river. She had been helping the servants wash the castle linens, but they had wandered off while the clothes were drying, and she could no longer even hear them.

She had her eyes closed and was smiling. "Then the king invited the whole kingdom to the ball," she whispered. She couldn't place exactly where she had read that, but remembered the drawing that went with it—

a huge room decorated with gaily-colored lanterns and crowded with young people dancing and laughing.

A cloud drifted over the sun and the air became uncomfortably chilly. Jennifer sat up and sighed.

It wasn't that her father wouldn't give a party for her—Jennifer was his only child and he doted on her. The problem was that there were so few people around who were her age. Young people had a tendency to drift away, looking for the chance to make their fortunes in larger, livelier kingdoms.

Jennifer sighed again. She sometimes felt that she had been born into a kingdom of old people and young children.

She sighed a third sigh, the loudest and longest yet, and then Jennifer turned her attention back to the laundry. She had just decided that one of her father's nightshirts needed further cleaning and was busily at work scrubbing when she heard someone approaching.

She looked up and saw the most splendid man she had ever seen anywhere, picture books included. He had curly golden hair, deep blue eyes, and very broad shoulders. His suit was gleaming white satin, and he had a marvelous maroon velvet cloak with fur trim. Everywhere about him there were flashes and sparkles as the sun reflected on gold buckles and rings.

His horse was white also, outfitted like its owner in maroon studded with gold. Both horse and rider carried themselves as if they expected to elicit breathless admiration.

Jennifer jumped to her feet and ran her hand through her hair. The stranger stopped several feet away from her and flashed a brilliant smile. "Hi, there. I'm Prince Alexander," he said, then added, "the king's son."

She could tell by the way he said it that he wasn't referring to a small woodland kingdom like her own, but one of the vast and mighty lands told of in song and story. She made an awkward curtsy while trying to keep her hand over one of the larger smudges on her dress.

The prince smiled graciously. "My horse seems to have lost a shoe. Could you tell me how to get to the nearest blacksmith?"

Jennifer finally remembered to breathe, then shook her head. "He's not here," she said. Then, seeing the prince's smile start to broaden at this obvious fact, she stammered, "I mean, he's not in town. He's gone on a fishing trip."

"Well, the second nearest, then," the prince suggested.

"I'm sorry, there's only the one. It's a small village," she added apologetically.

"I guess so. When will he be back?"

"Two days."

"Two?" the prince cried. "Days? Very unprofessional attitude there. What am I supposed to do?" He tapped his foot impatiently in its stirrup and glared at her.

Jennifer gulped. "I'm sorry. You'll just have to wait."

Alexander sighed loudly. "Is this village of yours

large enough to have an inn? I'll need a place to stay."

"Oh, I'm sure my father can find a room for you."

"He's the innkeeper?"

Jennifer looked down at her bare toes in the mud and said softly, "No, he's the king."

"Oh," the prince said, looking at her more closely than before. He cleared his throat. "Uhm, sorry." He smiled weakly and glanced away.

"Oh, no," she answered hastily, "the misunderstanding's all"—she looked away, afraid to see in his eyes the reflection of her drabness and the shabbiness of her surroundings— "my fault."

There were several seconds of silence before she introduced herself and added, "Here, I can show you the way up the hill to the castle."

She hurriedly threw the still-damp laundry into the wicker carrying basket, and Alexander nudged his horse out of her way as she scrambled up the slope that led back onto the road.

Jennifer tried to think of something clever to say. But she'd have to be quick, for she was rapidly running out of breath from the weight of the basket and trying to keep up with the pace of Alexander's horse. She finally decided to ask what brought him to her father's land. She didn't add that it was a rare occasion, indeed, when a stranger came through—and that when someone did, he was usually either lost or a traveling merchant or, in most cases, both.

"I'm looking for a wife," the prince said.

Now the idea of going about the countryside searching for a suitable bride was considered some-

"I'M LOOKING FOR A WIFE", THE PRINCE SAID.

what old-fashioned even back then, but Jennifer thought it was rather romantic, so she didn't say anything.

"You see," Alexander started and then interrupted himself. "You look like you're having trouble with that basket."

"Well, a bit," Jennifer admitted. Beside the fact that the basket was heavy, one wet sleeve of her father's nightshirt slapped the back of her leg with every step she took.

"Whoa, slow down," Alexander told the horse. "Genevieve can't keep up. Better?"

"Jennifer," she corrected, though she felt it was probably presumptuous to contradict such an obviously important person. "Yes, much better."

"You see," Alexander continued, "being the only son of the king—my father's the king, did I mention that?"

Jennifer nodded.

"Being the only son of the king, it's very important that I marry exactly the right person. And since I couldn't find exactly the right person in our own land, I've been traveling around the world to find her. No luck so far, though."

"It sounds very exciting," Jennifer said, picturing Prince Alexander in all the rich, exotic countries she had ever heard of. Then, looking up, she winced at the sight of the drafty old castle that was her home. "Well, here we are."

"Oh," said the prince, obviously disappointed. "How quaint."

"I'm sure we'll be able to find a very nice room for you."

The prince looked less than convinced, but didn't say so as Jennifer went to find her father and to change out of her damp, dirty work clothes.

Now it so happened that King Frederick was somewhat less impressed with their visitor than his daughter was, and he quickly tired of hearing Alexander say, "My father, the king, this . . ." and "My father, the king, that. . . ." So, anxious to be about his own business, he suggested that Jennifer and Alexander take a walk through the garden.

For his part, Alexander was not very enthusiastic, neither about the prospect of being stranded at the castle for a few days, nor about taking a walk in the garden with Jennifer. He had spent the last year visiting faraway lands meeting beautiful women from important families in fabulously rich cities. Quite frankly, Jennifer came nowhere near his high standards. But then, as a matter of fact, nobody did. On the other hand, there *was* the problem of the vacationing blacksmith. Even though a walk in the garden struck him as a rather dull way to pass the time, Jennnifer seemed like a nice enough person and a good listener, so Alexander agreed.

A Walk Through
the Enchanted Forest

A stone wall separated the forest from the castle garden. Jennifer walked in shy silence beside the wall as Alexander told her about his journey so far. Earlier he had talked of encountering vandals along the way. This had been smoothly changed to several reports of desperate thieves, and had now progressed to an armed gang of cutthroats shadowing him throughout the untamed wilderness. Then, abruptly, he stopped talking.

"What's this?" he asked, pointing to a metal gateway engraved with distorted figures who, with their large eyes and wild hair, looked ready to grasp at any passerby.

Jennifer shrugged. "It's just a gate leading into the forest."

"I can see that. But where does it go?"

"Nowhere. Just the forest," Jennifer said. "Come on, let's look at the garden."

Alexander walked up to the wall. "What a funny gate," he said, putting out his hand to touch one of the figures. But then he changed his mind and let his hand drop back to his side.

"It's always been here," Jennifer said, tugging gently on his arm. "But nobody goes through. It's locked and the key's been lost for as long as anyone can remember."

"Oh." Alexander, disappointed, tapped the door with his foot, and it swung open soundlessly.

Jennifer became very nervous. "I don't like this. The gate has always been locked before." Then she added, "The forest is enchanted."

Now this was not just idle guesswork on her part. There was a history book in the castle library that told how the wall had been built long ago to protect the people of the kingdom from the inhabitants of the forest. This book told of a time of unicorns and wishing wells and magic swords, when mysterious lights appeared in the night and strange people wandered about on secret journeys. Even then people had known that there was an evil force inside the forest, and kindly sorcerers had helped put up a wall that even the strongest magic could not tear down.

But now it was the fashion to scoff at magic. The history book about the enchanted forest was no longer taken seriously. Such foolish stories were put aside to make room for treatises on why the world was flat and how to improve the grain and corn crops. The wall remained only because it did no harm and because no one thought it worth the effort to tear down.

Jennifer was one of the few people who still believed in magic, but she usually didn't say so because people always laughed and called this belief "kid stuff."

Which is exactly what Alexander did now. The hint of adventure intrigued him, though, and he wanted to explore.

"But we don't know what's in there," Jennifer protested.

"All the more reason to explore. It'll be all right. I'll protect you."

"But it could be dangerous," she tried again.

"Nonsense," the prince answered, pulling her through the gateway. "I told you I don't believe in magic."

The door slammed shut behind them, and Alexander laughed confidently as Jennifer jumped.

"Just the wind," he said, starting down the well-cleared brick path.

Jennifer followed reluctantly.

Within a few minutes the wide path narrowed and tall trees laced their branches overhead, blocking out the sun. Chilled and unable to see well, Alexander quickly became bored; so after only a short walk they started back the way they had come. But they had gone only a few yards when they reached a fork in the road.

The prince scratched his head.

"That's odd," Jennifer said. "I don't remember the road dividing. Do you?"

"What? Oh, yes, of course it did. Didn't you notice? It was just about here."

"Oh," Jennifer said. "I must not have been paying attention. Which is the one that leads home?"

Alexander's hesitation lasted only two seconds. "Left," he declared decisively.

They had walked only a short distance when Jennifer stopped again. "Oh, dear," she said. The bricks had stopped and the road continued on as a narrow dirt path.

"Well, don't say I didn't tell you so," Alexander said.

"What?"

"I told you to take the other road, but you just started on down this way as if my opinion didn't matter at all."

Jennifer stamped her foot. "But you said left."

"I did not," Alexander protested. "I said right."

"You said left."

"Well, I meant to say right."

Jennifer sighed and started walking back without answering.

But although they walked and walked, they couldn't rediscover the fork in the road.

"Are we lost?" Jennifer asked.

"Lost?" Alexander's voice squeaked. "Of course we're not lost."

He sat down on a fallen tree next to the road. "But I'm too tired to walk anymore, so we'll just wait here until somebody comes along who can give us a ride back."

"But what if nobody does?"

"Somebody has to," Alexander reasoned. "Your father, for one, when we don't show up for supper."

"But he doesn't even know we're in the forest," Jennifer said. "We could wait here for days."

"*Days?*" Alexander squealed. "Don't say *days*."

"That's if they find us at all."

Alexander stood up angrily. "See what you've gotten me into," he snapped. "You and your crazy ideas. Let's explore the forest, indeed!"

"But . . ." Jennifer sputtered.

"Well, never mind. If we can't depend on your father, I'll have to rely on my own wits to get us out of this mess."

He started walking again.

"Oh, dear," Jennifer sighed.

The forest had been dark and gloomy all afternoon, but now, when they could see the sky through the trees, they could also see the moon, pale and small, low in the sky. Jennifer and Alexander began thinking about spending the night in the forest.

"This is incredible," Alexander said. "I'm a prince, not a squirrel. Princes don't sleep on the ground under trees. What would my father, the king, say?"

"I don't know," Jennifer answered, hoping he wouldn't become overly excited, "but what else is there to do?"

Alexander started to whine, but the sound turned to a whoop of joy. "Look!"

Jennifer clapped her hands in excitement, for there, just beyond some trees, was a little white cottage. "Oh, I do hope someone is home," she thought, for she noticed that all the curtains were drawn shut and no light came through any of them.

Alexander crossed the clearing in bounding strides, with Jennifer just a step behind.

"Aren't we going to knock?" she started as Alexander put his hand to the door. But by the time she had finished, he was already inside.

Jennifer followed more slowly.

The Cottage
in the Woods

It took several seconds for Jennifer's eyes to become accustomed to the dark. By then she had already guessed from the stillness that the house was empty.

"Anybody home?" Alexander called softly.

In the silence, Jennifer heard herself swallow.

Suddenly Alexander was standing behind her. "What's that?" he whispered, pointing over her shoulder with a trembling finger to a gleaming object on the wall facing them.

Jennifer tried to remind herself that this was nothing more than a dark house and took another step closer. She gave a sigh of relief. "It's only a mirror."

Alexander exhaled loudly. "That's what I thought."

The cottage was one rather large room divided in two by a fireplace that sat in the middle of the floor and was apparently used for both cooking and heating. The furniture, though there were only a few pieces, was surprisingly elegant, made of dark, heavy wood and ornately carved.

Jennifer and Alexander waited a long time for the owner of the cottage to return so they could ask for directions out of the forest. But as the time passed they began to worry that whoever it was might be on a long vacation and therefore would not be coming back at all that evening. So they made themselves at home, lit a fire, and cooked dinner.

Or rather, Alexander made himself at home while Jennifer lit a fire and cooked dinner because—as he told her—at home his father, the king, always had somebody around to do that sort of thing for him, and he didn't know how.

So he spent a good deal of time admiring himself in the mirror while she chopped the wood (he held the door for her), cooked a soup from vegetables she found in the cupboard (he complained that it took too long), and cleaned up (he had gone to lie down on the bed— just to rest his eyes for a second while they waited for the dishwater to heat over the fire—and had fallen asleep).

Finally finished, she tiptoed to the side of the bed and smiled down at him. In sleep, quiet for once, his face relaxed and handsome, Alexander looked incredibly helpless and lovable, and his faults were easier to ignore.

Jennifer took two blankets from the chest at the foot of the bed and gently draped one over the prince's slender form.

Then she wrapped the other blanket around her shoulders and went to a chair. With her toes tucked under the cushion for warmth, she was so tired that she fell asleep before she realized how uncomfortable her position was.

The Magic Mirror

Jennifer was in a rotten mood.

Normally her disposition was a model of pleasantness, but for the moment she was sweeping the floor with a fury that accomplished little more than sending clouds of dust skittering from one corner to the next.

Alexander, not aware that anything was wrong, sat on the corner of the table practicing disarming smiles in the large ornamental mirror that had startled them the night before. He tapped his foot to the vague melody he was humming.

"You don't need any help, do you?" he asked without turning to her.

Jennifer swept a pile of dust over the offending foot. Her bad mood had been caused by Alexander's insistence that they leave the house as soon as possible. Some time during the night it had occurred to him that the owner of the little cottage might be angry with them for taking over the place. The best way to avoid the owner's possible anger, Alexander had reasoned, was to avoid the owner.

But for her part, Jennifer had agreed to stay in the

house only after she had decided that there was nothing wrong with doing so. She didn't like the idea of slinking away into the woods as if they were guilty of something.

Besides, there were two advantages that she could name in waiting for the owner's return:

1. Whoever lived in the cottage hopefully knew the woods well enough to direct them on the way home.

2. They would have a chance to explain themselves and to assure the owner that someone from King Frederick's castle would be back to pay for all the firewood and food they had used.

Alexander, on the other hand, could counter these two points with three of his own:

1. He, Prince Alexander, could find his way out of any forest, enchanted or not, that had ever grown.

2. It is, after all, a great honor to have royalty visit, so he didn't see why anybody should be reimbursed for anything. And . . .

3. He had decided to take the mirror with him.

Now while Jennifer found his first reason privately doubtful and the second openly debatable, she could recognize in the third a downright criminal act when she heard one.

Alexander, however, was determined. He was constantly standing in front of the mirror (whether admiring it or himself was never actually all that clear), and he was sure that the owner would never willingly part with it.

No amount of arguing, pleading, or threatening had been able to convince him to leave without the mirror, and Jennifer was beginning to fear that if she made Alexander choose between her and the mirror, she would be left to find her own way home.

So now, as Alexander waited impatiently, Jennifer tidied up and tried to figure some way around the situation.

The prince gave the mirror his most dazzling smile. Then he reached over to take it off the wall.

"I wouldn't if I were you," a low voice warned.

Alexander whirled toward the door. It was still closed, and as far as he could tell, he and Jennifer were the only ones in the room.

"I said I'm taking the mirror, and that's that," he said.

Jennifer, who had heard nothing, looked up from making the bed.

"What?" she asked, pushing a long, dark strand of hair out of her eyes.

"I said, 'I'm taking the mirror, and that's that.' "

Jennifer was puzzled. "Yes, I know."

"All right." Alexander scowled as Jennifer gave him a funny look.

"All right," he repeated, reaching for the mirror.

"You'll be sorry," the same voice whispered.

"Now cut that out!"

Jennifer straightened up and put her hands on her hips. "Alexander, what is the matter with you?"

"Would you please stop telling me not to take the mirror?"

Jennifer sighed. "Well, you shouldn't, but I didn't say anything."

"Fine, just leave it at that." Alexander took a step forward.

"Third warning is the last."

This time she heard it, too. "Who said that?" she demanded.

"Oh, come on," Alexander chided. "Stop playing games."

"Who spoke?" she asked again.

"I did," the voice said.

Jennifer glanced around even though she was already certain that they were the only two in the room. "Where?" she asked.

"Here."

The voice seemed to be coming from the mirror. Jennifer looked at it doubtfully. "Here?"

"Of course. Do you see anybody else in the room?" the mirror laughed.

"Hey, that's pretty good," Alexander said to Jennifer. "How do you do that without moving your lips?"

Jennifer ignored him. "Who are you?" she asked the mirror.

"Let's just say I'm someone who wants to remain where he is."

Alexander laughed. "That's very clever."

"Alexander!" Jennifer cried. "I'm not doing anything! The mirror is talking!"

"Hi, there," Alexander said, trying to hold his lips together. "I'm a talking mirror. Who are you?"

"Really," she insisted, "it's not me."

The prince stepped closer to the mirror, grinning widely, but this time hardly moving his lips.

"Ds izha pdy gid tik efu no ha," he announced.

Jennifer raised her eyebrows at him.

Alexander looked disappointed. "I said, 'This is a pretty good trick if you know how.'"

"Alexander." Jennifer put her hand on his arm and looked directly into his eyes. "This is no trick. I am not talking for the mirror. Now, Mirror, say something."

The mirror cawed and whistled like a parrot. "The prince is a jerk."

"Wait a minute," Alexander said.

"Did you see my lips move at all?" Jennifer asked. "Did the voice even come from this spot?"

Alexander looked around in bewilderment. "No," he admitted slowly. "But if you aren't talking, who is?"

"The mirror is." Jennifer was becoming impatient.

Alexander wore a look that said he couldn't be convinced that easily. "But a mirror can't talk."

"A magic mirror could."

"But there's no such thing as magic," he protested.

The mirror cawed and whistled again.

"You, be quiet." Alexander stood defiantly glaring at the mirror. "There is," he repeated slowly and deliberately, "no such thing as magic."

"The prince is a jerk," the mirror repeated.

"Someone is playing a trick on us!" Alexander bellowed, dashing to the door. He flung it open. No one was there.

Jennifer watched him spend the next several minutes running around the cottage, alternating directions in an attempt to catch whoever he figured had to be out there. Finally she went outside to look for him, and the prince, edging craftily around a corner, found himself nose-to-nose with her. Each gasped loudly.

"Would you stop fooling around?" she pleaded.

Alexander growled an answer she couldn't understand and slunk back inside.

"Anyone out there?" the mirror asked.

"No," Alexander admitted.

"Too bad."

"You are not magic!" Alexander insisted, crossing his arms over his chest and looking as though he felt just a bit silly addressing a mirror. "There is no such thing as magic. I've never seen a witch fly by on a broomstick, or an alchemist change lead to gold, or a frog turn out to be anything but a frog. Those things just can't happen."

"Lesson One," the mirror said: "Don't disbelieve something just because you can't see it."

"You're a fraud!" Alexander cried. "I believe in what I can see. And there's nothing you can do to keep me from taking you with me."

Before he had a chance to make even a slight move toward the wall, there was a bright flash. It was as though the mirror had caught the reflection of the noon sun, magnified it, and flung it back at them.

Jennifer threw her hands up to cover her face and squeezed her eyes shut.

She was still in that position when Alexander lowered the arm he had tried to shield his eyes with and blinked roughly several times.

"Now you can't see *anything*," the mirror said when

it was sure Alexander had caught on to the situation. "What do you believe in now?"

Jennifer lowered her suddenly cold hands and looked into the prince's blinded face. Trembling, she saw his expression change from frightened surprise to outrage.

"How dare you!" Alexander said in a quavering voice that became louder with each word. "You can't do this to me!"

"There is," the mirror said, "such a thing as magic."

"Do you have any idea who I am?" Alexander shouted, shaking Jennifer's hand off his shoulder. "My father is the king!"

The mirror remained calm. "Witches *do* fly on broomsticks, lead *is* turned to gold, and more princes than you would care to hear about spend their lives squatting on lily pads snapping up flies."

Alexander put out his hand to steady himself and blundered against the table. "Give me back my sight."

"I am a magic mirror."

"Give me back my sight."

"I am a magic mirror."

Alexander's hand tightened around the teakettle. "You are nothing!" he screamed, and hurled the kettle at the mirror.

There was a sharp bang, followed by a yell from Alexander as though he had dealt himself the blow; then there was a clinking, chinking, tinkling noise as if the glass were also crying out.

From the spot where the kettle had hit, Jennifer could see cracks spreading like a crazy cobweb—

branching out, meeting, dividing, covering the entire surface of the mirror until it was separated into a thousand shimmering pieces. And in each piece, she saw Alexander's mouth form the same wordless cry as he staggered back and sank slowly, slowly down. Then, with a last crystalline sigh, the countless tiny mirrors released these images and let them join the prince on the floor.

Jennifer stood unable to move until the glassy whispers had faded. Even then, her legs felt weighted down and she was afraid to try walking.

"Alexander," she said softly, reaching out to him.

He remained sprawled motionless on the floor, his eyes closed.

"Is he dead?" Jennifer wondered out loud.

"So it seems," came a steady voice at her side, "but so it is not."

Jennifer spun around to face the mirror, ready to accuse, eager to demand explanations. Her own reflection glowered back at her—dark eyes in a pale face that frowned more deeply as she realized the mirror was whole again. No smashed center, no jagged cracks—the mirror twinkled and shone in amusement.

"He's not dead?" Jennifer asked suspiciously.

"Asleep."

"How can I wake him?"

"A kiss usually works."

Jennifer was surprised to find that she could walk after all. She knelt beside Alexander and softly kissed his cold lips.

JENNIFER COULD SEE CRACKS SPREAD... ...ING LIKE A MANIAC COBWEB

Nothing happened.

"A kiss usually works," the mirror said, "but not always."

Jennifer felt the same sort of frustration building in her that had probably led Alexander to smash the mirror. "What, then?"

"Don't you know?" The mirror's surprise sounded nowhere near genuine.

Jennifer shook her head.

The mirror made a clucking noise. "Lesson Two: If the answer isn't in you, it isn't."

"But what *is* the answer?" she demanded, jumping to her feet.

"Well, it's not impatience."

Jennifer stamped her foot.

"And it's not anger, either." The mirror's tone was becoming harder. "Why don't you think about it for a while," it suggested, then suddenly snapped, "but not here. You're beginning to bore me. I might decide to put a spell on you, too, any second now."

Jennifer backed toward the door.

"Yes," the mirror considered, "any . . . second . . . NOW!"

Jennifer turned and ran out the door, down the cobblestone path, through the gate, and into the forest.

Inside the cottage, the mirror continued to twinkle and shine in the morning sunlight.

And the prince slept.

The Old Witch

She was simply called the Old Witch.

She was called this by those who lived in the enchanted forest, and by those who had built the magic wall to keep the forest where it belonged, and by all the dark, formless creatures who rode the wind on long, moonless nights.

Since as long as anyone could remember she had lived in a cave whose inside few had ever seen. The cave was filled with the smell of rotting leaves never swept out from autumns long past and with the sound of water dripping down slimy walls to form murky puddles on the rough floor. For anyone who dared to peek inside, there was an assortment of cobweb-covered jars and boxes containing secret things, a foul-smelling caldron that bubbled thickly day and night throughout the years, and several species of mushrooms growing in the darkest corners. There was also a hand-embroidered picture that bore the message HOME SWEET HOME.

For the moment the cave's only occupants were the spiders, bats, and silent, slippery things that always live in such places. The Old Witch had gone outside because her magic pool had warned that someone was approaching.

"Who?" the Old Witch had demanded peevishly. "Don't just say, 'Someone's coming,' you fool. Show me who."

The pool's surface had shimmered briefly, then showed the features of a young girl's face.

"Well, she just better not," the Old Witch had cackled. "If she knows what's good for her, she better just steer clear of us." With that she had gone to crouch behind a big rock to get a better look.

Jennifer, unaware either of what was good for her or that she was being watched, spotted not the cave but the clear stream that flowed beside it.

The Old Witch saw Jennifer change direction and softly hissed, "Go on, little trespasser, go on. Keep away from our cave. The magic pool and I, we don't like visitors. We don't like you."

But, of course, she was too far away to be heard, and Jennifer stooped beside the water's edge and cupped her hands for a drink.

When she was finished, the young girl sighed and looked around. She had been wandering, lost and frightened, for several hours and still was no closer to finding her way out of the forest than she had been that morning. She wanted to rest but decided to keep going. The sooner she got back to the castle, the sooner she could bring back help for Prince Alexander. She thought of his handsome face and his impossible manner, and shook her head, wishing there was someone else around who could handle this.

"What?" the Old Witch murmured. "Leaving already? Has she seen our cave? Is she going to try to get into our home?"

Jennifer had indeed seen the cave, but she definitely had no intention of going anywhere near it, and started back toward the path.

The Old Witch jumped up from her hiding place. "You better not!" she screamed.

Jennifer whirled to face the old woman, whose black clothes flapped like a scarecrow's in the wind.

After what had happened with the mirror, she was very sensitive about following instructions. "What?" she asked anxiously. "I better not what?"

"You better not go near our cave."

Jennifer glanced at the dark hole in the side of the hill that she had noticed before. "But I wasn't," she protested. "I was walking the other way entirely."

The Old Witch glared at her suspiciously. "Well, you just be careful, that's all. Get out of here now."

Jennifer took a few steps backward to put more distance between them. "There's nothing I'd like better," she said. "You see, I'm lost."

"Well, you shouldn't have gotten lost near our cave."

"Honestly, I never intended to. If you could just tell me how to get out of the forest—"

"*Out of the forest!*" the Old Witch hooted. "Did you hear that? She wants to get out of the forest!"

Jennifer peered around, wondering to whom the old woman was talking. When she looked back, the other's face was up close to her own.

"Nobody gets out of the forest, little one."

"Oh, dear," Jennifer said. "But I need to get some help."

The Old Witch spat on the ground and asked, "What for?"

"To break a spell."

"To break a spell? 'To break a spell,' she says!" The Old Witch had a very shrill voice that hurt Jennifer's ears, but the young girl nodded. "*I* could break the spell."

"You could?"

"I could, girlie. I am absolutely, positively, undeniably the most powerful witch that ever was, that ever will be, or that ever could be. I can make spells, I can break spells, I can . . ." The Old Witch stopped because she couldn't think of anything else she could do with a spell. "Well, anyway, I can. What do you think of that?"

"I'm impressed," Jennifer admitted, which was certainly true. "Will you help me?"

"I don't think so. But we'll see." The Old Witch started walking toward the cave. "Come on, come on. Don't dawdle," she called, and Jennifer reluctantly followed.

She had only taken one step into the cave when the Old Witch whirled to face her. "Want an apple, sweetie?" she asked, pulling a big, shiny red fruit out from within the yards of her black clothes.

Jennifer hesitated. She hadn't eaten since breakfast, but she wasn't sure she cared to trust the witch. On the other hand, she didn't dare offend her either.

"Maybe I'll have one later," she hedged.

"Maybe I won't offer you one later." With her few yellow teeth the witch took a big, juicy bite out of the apple, while watching Jennifer's reaction with her glowing equally-yellow eyes. "Good instincts for a young whippersnapper," she announced, tossing the rest of the fruit over her shoulder. "Knows enough not to eat while she's in an enchanted place. Or is she just afraid to take food from a stranger? Who cares anyway? Sit down, little dumpling, sit down. Tell me about this spell I could break with a snap of my fingers if I chose to."

Jennifer started from the beginning—describing Alexander.

This was a mistake. The Old Witch made an ugly, snorting noise. *"Handsomest man in the world,"* she mocked. "What do you know about it?"

"Well, he's the handsomest man I ever saw."

The Old Witch made a nasty sound and ordered Jennifer to the side of what looked like just another of many large puddles on the floor. "Now describe him very carefully."

Jennifer thought this a bit peculiar, but she began to do as she had been instructed. She was interrupted by the witch screaming, "Well, come on, you stupid fool, come on! What do you think we're waiting for?"

Jennifer looked up, but saw that the witch seemed to be addressing the floor. "Please, ma'am," she asked meekly, "who are you talking to?"

"Who do you think, you silly thing?" the Old Witch snapped. "The pool. The magic pool."

"Oh," Jennifer said, and looked back to see a vague form in the water.

"We go back a long time together, the pool and I, don't we?" the Old Witch murmured. "Yes, we do, and now we'll see if this prince of hers is the handsomest man in the world. Go on, pumpkin, go on."

Jennifer began to describe Alexander, and the more she described him, the clearer his picture became in the magic pool.

"Is that him?" the hag asked impatiently. "Is this what you think the handsomest man in the world looks like? Well, he's not bad, I'll grant you that. And I'll wager he's the best a silly young thing like you could find. But he's nothing compared to my beau. Is he now?"

Jennifer wasn't prepared to argue the point, but in any case the witch wasn't talking to her but to the pool.

"Come on, then. Show the child our beau. Come on, come on, you slow thing. There! I wonder what she thinks now. I wonder if she still thinks her prince is the handsomest man in the world."

Jennifer cleared her throat. Now the man whose picture was in the pool was very handsome, there was no denying that. He looked like the kind of dark, mysterious stranger that fortune-tellers are so partial to. Only it just so happened that Jennifer preferred Alexander's blond-haired, blue-eyed, smiling face. "Well, this man certainly is quite handsome," she admitted.

"Yes?"

"Very intense eyes."

"WELL, THIS MAN CERTAINLY IS QUITE HANDSOME," SHE ADMITTED.

"Very," the witch agreed. "And?"

"And he seems quite tall and athletic."

"But what else?"

"What else? Ahm." Jennifer's mind had gone blank and she groped for something to say. "His clothes are very interesting. I've never seen anything quite like them. Does he come from some other country?"

Again, this was the wrong thing to say. The Old Witch brought her foot down sharply at the edge of the pool. When the ripples settled, the picture was gone. "So they're old-fashioned, so what?"

"I'm sorry," Jennifer said, although she wasn't sure what had happened.

"I haven't seen him in awhile, but he's coming back."

"Oh," Jennifer said, simply to say something.

"*Oh,*" the Old Witch mimicked. "*Oh.* She thinks she can make fun of my beau just because he isn't here, does she? The pert little thing thinks she's clever just because we haven't seen my beau in awhile. But we know he's coming back, don't we?"

"I'm sure he is," Jennifer said, edging toward the cave mouth. "I—"

"*I'm sure he is,*" the witch echoed. "You what? You think he never planned to come back? You think he wouldn't come back to me? Well, I was young and pretty once. Younger than you and prettier than you. We'll see who gets whose beau back first, won't we? If she even has one. If she didn't make him up."

"No, you don't understand. He's not my beau," Jennifer started, but the magic pool was shifting and shimmering again. With a description of Alexander, it had been able to locate him in the enchanted forest and now showed him as Jennifer had left him, asleep under the mirror.

The Old Witch's annoyance at seeing that there really was such a person dissolved with a hiss as she ran a skinny hand through her gray hair. "Malveenya's cottage. The two young fools have gotten mixed up with Malveenya's magic, have they?" She turned to Jennifer and started pushing her closer to the exit. "Get out. We're not going to tinker with Malveenya's spells. Now get out. You have no right to be in our cave anyway."

"But who's Malveenya?" Jennifer asked.

"*Who?*" the witch cried. " '*Who? Who?* ' she asks. Who do you think they were so afraid of that they built the magic wall? Who do you think they were trying to keep in here? Silly girl, get out of here. Forget your prince, and leave me alone."

She had pushed Jennifer outside the cave and shoved her in the direction she had been going in earlier.

"And don't come back!" she screamed as the young girl took a few uncertain steps.

Jennifer watched as the Old Witch angrily stamped back into the cave. There were so many things left unsaid. Jennifer had never meant to hint that the dark young man didn't intend to come back. She wanted to apologize for giving that impression. Also, she wanted to find out more about this Malveenya and how powerful she really was.

Jennifer quietly stole up to the cave mouth and looked in.

The Old Witch was striding about. "Stupid girl," she mumbled. "Stupid pool, stupid beau. Who needs you? Who needs anybody? I think I'll drain the water out of you, Magic Pool; you're a health hazard anyway." She stood tapping her foot. "I never want to see his face again. Do you hear that? Never again."

She stamped around a bit longer while Jennifer tried to decide if she really wanted to go in. She had just decided yes when the Old Witch said, "I've changed my mind. Let me see him again." She tapped her foot impatiently. "I said, 'Let me see him again.'"

When she got no answer, the Old Witch sank to her knees and pleaded. "I'm sorry, Magic Pool. I didn't mean that about draining you. I like the mosquitoes in summer and the ice in winter. I wouldn't really drain you. Are you still there?"

The pool gave a slight shimmer.

"We go back together a long time, you and I, don't we?" the Old Witch sighed.

The pool shimmered again, and from where she stood Jennifer could see the dark young man's face reappear.

The Old Witch still hadn't moved several minutes later, when Jennifer turned to make her way back to the road.

The Sorcerer

Jennifer continued down the road for a very short way before she came to another woodland cottage.

Her first impression was that the place was deserted, for it was rather rundown, with weeds successfully invading the vegetable garden, and a broken shutter hanging loose against the side of the house. But then she noticed a well slightly off to one side and a young man pulling up the bucket.

She came up behind him, intending to introduce herself. "Excuse me," she said.

He gave a startled gasp and jumped back. The bucket clattered down into the depths of the well.

Jennifer opened her mouth to apologize when, to her surprise, the person standing before her was suddenly gone and she found herself addressing a hawthorn bush.

"That's odd," she thought, circling the bush, which was shaking violently despite the fact that there was no wind.

When she could find no trace of the young man, she started toward the house to see if she could find some help there.

Suddenly she changed her mind. "I saw what I saw," she told herself, and quickly turned back to the well. She was in time to see an old man with a long white beard trying to tiptoe out of the clearing into the forest. There was no sign of the hawthorn bush.

"Stop!" she called, and the old man froze, then slowly and quietly peeked at her over his shoulder to see if she were talking to him. When he saw that she was, he came back to the center of the clearing.

"How did you do that?" she demanded.

"Do what?" the old man asked, trying to act casual and leaning over the well to pull up the bucket.

"You changed!"

"All life is a series of changes."

"Yes, but just now, this very minute. You were about my age not thirty seconds ago, and then you were a bush. You're a sorcerer, aren't you?" Normally Jennifer wouldn't have been so bold, but the fact that he seemed so nervous made her feel that he wasn't to be feared. Besides, the events of that morning had made her desperate.

"I what? No, of course I'm not! What an imagination you have, little girl."

That was the wrong thing to call her. "I'm not a little girl. And I know what I saw."

"Nonsense," the sorcerer replied, walking toward his house. "How nice of you to drop by. You must come again some day soon." He slammed the door behind him.

Jennifer knocked on the door. "Sir?" she called. "Sir, could I talk with you?"

There was no answer from inside the cottage. Jennifer wondered what she had said to cause this to happen.

She put her face close to the glass part of the door and tried to peek around the edge of the curtain.

She found a fierce gray eye peeking back at her.

Both girl and sorcerer jumped back in surprise. Then he gave the curtain an angry tug and Jennifer could hear him stamp away from the door.

She knocked again. "Yoo-hoo," she cried.

No answer.

She put her ear to the door, but all she could hear was her own breathing.

Suddenly the door flew open and Jennifer half-fell into the room.

"Would you please go away?" the old man hissed.

"Not until you help me." Jennifer forced herself to stand straight and look him directly in the eyes, but she was trembling inside and trying to remember what had made her think he was nervous.

"I said, 'Go away!' " the sorcerer bellowed, suddenly transformed into a seven-foot Viking warrior, which left Jennifer at eye level with a bear-tooth necklace low on his chest.

She looked up—again into his eyes. She was beginning to become angry. "You have terrible manners," she said softly.

The sorcerer scowled but slowly shrank back to normal size. By the time they were face-to-face, he was a young man again.

"So what?" He didn't sound angry, but, then again, he didn't sound friendly either.

Jennifer was too angry to worry about how he felt. "I've come to you for help, and you're playing games and being unfriendly and rude and trying to scare me away, and I think that's terrible!"

The sorcerer looked at her coldly. Now that he was standing still, Jennifer noticed for the first time that he was slightly shorter than she was; but the power she sensed in him made her tremble. She became angry with herself when she saw he noticed her shaking.

It was the sorcerer who gave in and lowered his eyes first.

"My apologies," he murmured, holding a flower that hadn't been there a second before.

Instinctively, Jennifer reached out; but the flower was gone before her fingers could grasp it.

The sorcerer was showing her to the door. "But I *am* busy, and you *have* invaded my privacy."

"But who can help me?" Jennifer pleaded.

"City hall?" the sorcerer suggested. "A doctor? The cavalry? The high lama of Tibet?"

"No, no, no, no," Jennifer said. "I need you."

"Then you're out of luck," the sorcerer answered, closing the door quietly behind her.

Jennifer sat silently on the step.

After a minute or so, the door opened again.

"Just how long do you plan on sitting there?" the sorcerer asked.

Jennifer didn't answer, and he slammed the door

shut again. A few seconds later he opened it. "What makes you think I could help you even if I wanted to?" he shouted.

Still Jennifer didn't answer.

The sorcerer stooped down beside her. "Go home," he whispered.

"I can't," Jennifer said.

He considered this for a moment. "Lost?"

Jennifer nodded. "That's part of it."

The sorcerer sighed and ran his fingers through his frizzy red hair. "Okay," he said gently, "you can come in and have some tea, and then I'll show you the way out of the forest."

Jennifer started to interrupt, but the sorcerer talked over her objections. "I don't want to hear the rest of it. That's all I'm going to do. I'm not interested in who you are or why you're here. I don't care what your problems are. Tea and the road out. Is that clear?"

"Don't you even want to know my name?"

"Oh, no you don't!" the sorcerer warned. "I especially don't want to hear that. I'm not interested. Don't tell me."

"But why?" Jennifer asked.

"Because if I know your name, you'll become a real person to me. Then, whenever I hear that name, I'll think of you, remember the afternoon we shared tea, and wonder whatever happened to you. I don't want to get involved. I'm no good with people. I don't get to see a lot of them, here in the forest, and I like it that way. So, whatever your problems are, they're *your* problems. I don't want to know your name and I don't

want to know you. Do you understand what I'm saying?"

"Yes."

"Good."

"It's Jennifer."

The sorcerer glared at her.

Jennifer smiled. It was the smile she usually saved
for her father when he was angry. It was slow and
unsure and eventually turned into a sad little frown
with downcast eyes.

This last part, however, made it hard for Jennifer to
tell what kind of reaction it was getting.

She could hear the sorcerer stand up. When she finally looked at him, his face had not softened; but he
stood by the open door waiting for her.

He sighed as she came in. "Mine's Norman," he said.

Norman

The cottage was bright and cheery but so cluttered that it was hard to move about.

The young sorcerer gathered a pile of books and papers off the table and put them on a nearby chair. Then, realizing that he had now filled the only available chair in the house, he picked them back up and looked around helplessly before adding them to an already tilting stack of boxes on the floor.

Jennifer sat on the edge of her seat to keep from leaning on the unfolded laundry draped over the back.

He removed a potted geranium from the top of a little three-legged stool and, still holding the plant, pulled the stool closer to Jennifer.

"Now, Jennifer," he said, "tell me again."

She had already explained everything that had happened since she first met Alexander, but she started over.

"With the mirror," he interrupted. "You're leaving something out there."

"What?"

He gave her a disappointed look. "If I knew that,

would I need you to tell me?" He kept changing all the while they were talking—short to tall to old to young. At the moment he was about her father's age and had given himself less kinky hair.

Jennifer wasn't sure if it would be polite to comment on all this, but she found it most distracting.

Norman was still talking. "You see, there has to be a way to break the spell; and by the rules of magic, the mirror had to tell you how." He held up a hand to forestall her objection. "It might not have told you clearly, but it did tell you."

Jennifer thought that over for a while. "Oh, like a riddle." He nodded, and Jennifer watched, fascinated, while he made a strange motion, chewing on air, with his hand close to but not touching his mouth. Seeing her expression, he suddenly remembered that he didn't currently have a beard and tapped his teeth instead.

"Let's go over everything you can remember the mirror saying," Norman suggested.

They did, several times. But again and again they found themselves facing two ideas that seemed most likely to hold the key, but that they couldn't decipher.

The first was when the mirror had said, "Lesson One: Don't disbelieve something just because you can't see it." ("A valid point," Norman admitted, "though it's too bad the mirror felt obliged to prove it.")

Lesson Two was bothersome to the young sorcerer: "If the answer isn't in you, it isn't."

"Well," Norman reasoned, "if it's in *you*, then it can't very well be in *me*."

That sounded distressingly like he was still trying to

"LET'S GO OVER EVERYTHING YOU CAN REMEMBER, THE MIRROR SAYING."

get out of helping her, so Jennifer quickly asked, "Are you going to tell me about Malveenya?"

"I've never actually met her, but from what I hear she's extremely powerful and has a temper that would make that mirror of hers seem gentle as a month-old bunny."

"Oh," the girl said.

"I gather she likes to use pain and fear on helpless creatures—not necessarily to get her own way, but just because she likes to."

Jennifer gulped and decided she didn't really want to know any more about Malveenya. "Is there anything we can do about Alexander?" she asked instead.

"Okay," Norman considered. "Malveenya has several places around the forest. Apparently she was away from the cottage and the mirror was simply acting on its own to defend itself. If you had left it alone, it wouldn't have bothered you."

Jennifer gave him an apologetic half-smile.

"The fact that the mirror was acting on its own, without Malveenya's power, means that maybe the spell is weak enough to be countered."

Jennifer jumped up from her chair. "You can break the spell?"

Norman stood up also and immediately added an extra foot to his height. "Not with the information you gave me, and not if Malveenya's gotten in on the act."

He replaced the geranium on the stool and started pacing about the room as Jennifer sank back down with a little "Oh." She watched his hair turn to auburn and a bushy mustache appear, and she asked, "Why do you keep doing that?"

Norman stopped pacing. "What?" he asked.

"You keep changing."

"Ahm, no, actually I don't. Appearances are deceiving. Things are not necessarily what they seem."

While Jennifer tried to figure out what that had to do with anything, Norman suddenly took on the form of a large eagle furiously flapping his wings. "I can change my appearance, but not my reality," he said, his voice the same as always. "I may look like an eagle, but I can't fly. I could make you think I look like a gazelle"—he demonstrated—"but that doesn't mean I can run any faster than I could if I looked like a fish." He showed her this, too, then returned to his form as a skinny red-haired youth.

"And I could stay looking like a fish all day, since I wouldn't need to be in the water, whereas if I stuck my head in the well long enough, I'd drown whether that head seemed to belong to a speckled trout or to a hippopotamus."

"I get the point," Jennifer said quickly, before he took it upon himself to show her what he'd look like as a hippopotamus.

Norman held out his hand to show her the large ring he was wearing. The edges showed gold, but mostly it was a wide band of dark blue with glittering little stars.

"This is how I do it. The sorcerer who used to live here gave me this magic ring before he retired. He probably could have helped you a lot better. I'm very young for a sorcerer, and I don't have much experience. This ring's the only magic I have, and I certainly don't see how it can possibly help us against Malveenya."

"Us?" Jennifer said hopefully.

Norman usually wore a very serious expression that often bordered on looking downright sad, but now he gave her a smile. "Us," he assured her.

Again
the Old Witch

Jennifer was sitting on a wide, flat-topped rock watching the patterns caused by the current as the water met and flowed around her feet dangling in the stream.

Norman was lying on the ground several yards away from the cave entrance, nose-to-nose with a curious rabbit.

An old shoe came flying out of the cave. It didn't land anywhere near them but it startled the rabbit, who first crouched close to the ground and then stood on its back legs, sniffing the air and quivering its ears. In another second it disappeared into the tall grass.

"I said, 'Nobody's home!' " the Old Witch's creaky voice screamed at them. "Now scram!"

"Just a few minutes of your time," Norman called without turning to face the cave. They had been going through this for some time now, and the shoe was only one of several furious, if somewhat inaccurately aimed, missiles scattered on the grass in front of the witch's home.

"Go away, you young hoodlums!"

· 48 ·

Norman sighed. "Please. We only want to talk."

"I have nothing to say to you."

"A simple business transaction."

"Drop dead."

"I'm sure we can work something out."

There was no further sound from the cave, and Jennifer concentrated her attention on a smooth pebble that she examined with her toe.

According to Norman, the Old Witch owned something that might be able to help them: a jinni in a bottle.

"Oh!" Jennifer had cried eagerly upon hearing this, for she had great faith in the value of magic. "Do you think she'll let us use it?"

"Not likely," Norman had answered. "You know how ornery she can be. And don't get too excited, it's only good for one wish. But, it's worth a try."

So far, though, their try wasn't going very well. Neither Norman nor Jennifer wanted to force their way in, and the Old Witch refused to come out. She would stand well inside, yelling at them and throwing whatever she thought might inflict bodily harm.

Happily, though, the intervals between these episodes were rapidly shortening as curiosity wore her down. ("Just the way you wore me down," Norman noted, but Jennifer decided against responding to that.)

"You're juvenile delinquents!" the Old Witch called.

"No, we're not," Norman answered. "We just want to talk to you."

"About what?"

That took both young people by surprise.

"No, stay back," she warned from the doorway as they jumped to their feet and started toward the cave. "We can talk from here. What do you want?"

"Your jinni in the bottle," Norman started, but she cut him off with a sharp laugh.

"Ha, do you hear that? It's our magic bottle they want. Well, they aren't going to get it, are they? No, I didn't think so. Good-bye, and good riddance."

"No, wait. I'm not just asking for a hand-out. I thought we could talk about a trade."

The Old Witch took one step out of the doorway. A breeze lifted her wispy gray hair as she narrowed her yellow eyes at them. But she also made a motion with her head, telling him to go on.

"I thought maybe I could give you something for the bottle."

"Sounds good," the witch said. "I'll take your magic ring."

"Are you out of your mind?" Norman cried.

"You said trade. Didn't he say trade? That's the only thing you have that I'm interested in."

"I had in mind something more like my services," the sorcerer explained, hastily regaining his composure. "Like mowing your lawn or painting your cave or something."

"We like our lawn the way it is, don't we, Magic Pool? And the cave doesn't need painting. I'll take your ring."

"Look, let's be reasonable. You've already made your own wish. The bottle isn't any good to you anymore."

The witch shook her head. "But we've grown very

fond of it as a decorative piece. It fits in perfectly with the living room's motif."

"What?" Norman said.

"You heard. That's our final offer."

Norman glanced at Jennifer, who hadn't said a word but wore an expression that said all her hopes in the world were being destroyed. "Wait," he called, to keep the Old Witch from leaving as he frantically tried to think of something.

She saw the dejected look on Jennifer's face and said coolly, "Isn't it worth your magic ring to help out this young lady?"

"Don't do it," Jennifer whispered. "We'll find some other way."

Norman continued speaking to the old woman, trying to keep his voice even. "Look, the ring isn't all that great. All it can do is change your appearance. Wouldn't it be better to have me around to chop wood for you on cold winter days, or to build a well so you wouldn't have to come down the hill to the stream, or—?"

"No."

"Pick anything else. You can have all my books."

"I don't like books."

"I'll share all the incantations I know and I'll show you all my secret formulas."

The Old Witch looked bored. "I've got enough of my own."

"I'll give you my whole house."

"Would you get off my back? I already told you there's nothing wrong with the cave. Now face up to it—I want your ring or it's no deal."

Norman motioned to her to wait and pulled Jennifer aside. "What do you think?" he asked. "She sounds pretty definite about the ring."

Jennifer nodded. "If that's all she'll settle for, then we'll have to do without the jinni."

"I'm afraid it's not going to be that easy. Getting the jinni to help us isn't our best plan; it's our *only* plan."

"But the ring is your base of power—"

The sorcerer scratched his red hair. "It may be a base of power, but it's a very narrow base. I haven't gotten much use out of it. And I know she can't do any harm with it."

"Norman!" Jennifer said.

He patted her hand. "If the jinni is a powerful one, maybe he can help us in more ways than one."

"But you said we'll only get one wish."

"Right. But the trick is to make that one wish count for a lot."

"It doesn't look like that jinni helped the Old Witch very much," the girl said, glancing at the cave.

"Hey, we heard that!" the Old Witch hollered. "You just mind your own business, missy."

"I wonder what she wished for," Jennifer whispered, as she and the sorcerer approached the cave again.

"Well, from what I've heard, the jinni had a very thick accent," Norman said, imitating the way a Middle Eastern jinni might speak. "And while he was explaining the rules, the Old Witch stamped her foot and said"—and here he mimicked her creaky voice—" 'I wish you'd stop talking with that stupid accent,' and that, as they say, was that." He gave a wide grin and the Old Witch spat on the ground.

"Nobody likes a smart-mouth kid," she said.

Norman instantly put on his old face with the long white beard and gave a low bow. "Anything that'll make you happy."

The Old Witch scratched herself noisily, then spat again. "Yeah, well, let's see this tricky ring of yours before we make any final decisions."

The sorcerer pulled the ring off and handed it to her. She immediately slipped it onto her finger and went through a dizzying series of changes so quickly that Jennifer couldn't tell what she saw, but she was pretty sure that at one point it was an Egyptian pharaoh and at another a rather pudgy duckling.

"Not bad," the witch said, resuming her former face. "Wait here for a second."

Norman gave Jennifer a tight smile and tugged on his beard.

The Old Witch came out almost immediately and tossed a plain brown bottle toward them. Norman coughed at the dust that flew as he grabbed it.

"There you go," she said, turning back to her cave. "Thanks a lot."

"Wait a minute," Jennifer said, a sudden awful feeling in her throat.

Norman was a bit slower to catch on because he was examining the old bottle and hadn't seen her movement. "Does this mean it's a deal?"

"Now you've got it, sweetie," the witch answered.

"I thought we could talk to the jinni first to see if he's what we need."

"Nope."

Norman knit his bushy white eyebrows in annoyance, but accepted this. "All right, then. Just give me back my ring so I can turn myself back to normal, and then it's all yours."

"Nope."

He took a step forward, trying to reason with her. "Look, you can trust me. Here, you can hold the bottle while I've got the ring."

The witch wouldn't touch the bottle. "A deal's a deal."

Jennifer saw the sorcerer's face grow pale. "Now, wait a minute. You said you just wanted to see the ring."

"Did I?" the old woman said sweetly. "You must have misunderstood me."

"Old Witch, I've been acting in good faith! This isn't fair!"

She examined the edge of her torn sleeve that had been dragged through chicken stew last week and which she hadn't gotten around to cleaning yet. "Since when has life been fair?" she hooted. "Now get away from our cave."

Norman was furious. "You can't do this!"

Suddenly he was confronting a gigantic purple dragon who blew a flame seven feet long. He took an instinctive step backward before remembering it was only an illusion.

"Wrong, sorcerer," the dragon said, her yellow eyes smoldering. "I can do whatever I want." She executed a graceful turn and disappeared into the cave. Her voice carried out to them as she called, "Defensive wall."

Neither Jennifer nor Norman saw or heard anything happen, but when they tried to follow her into the cave, they found they couldn't. There was some sort of unseen barrier through which they were unable to pass. It reached from the ground to as high as their fingers could stretch and fit into every jagged nook of the entryway. As clear as the air around them, as hard as the rock of the cave—there was no getting around it and no getting through it.

They could hear the witch singing, "La-la-la-la-de-dah," inside.

Norman kicked at a stone, which bounced off the invisible wall and almost hit him. "How could I be so stupid?" he demanded.

Jennifer thought it was one of those trick questions that doesn't really have a right answer, so she didn't try to give one, but said instead, "That was mean and sneaky and underhanded," which seemed like something no one could argue with.

Norman made a low, growling sound in the back of his throat. "And I should have expected it." He looked around for something to throw, then remembered the bottle he had put down in order to examine the wall. "Well, at least we still have this."

"Do you think it's the right bottle?"

He gave his beard a good hard tug. "Well, there's one sure way to find out."

The Jinni

Jennifer picked up the bottle.

She had never seen a jinni's bottle before and hadn't really known what to expect, but she was surprised anyway. Underneath a heavy coating of sticky dust, it appeared to be an ordinary glass container.

She blew off some of the dust, but couldn't see through the thick brown glass. She looked over to Norman and took a deep breath. Then she pulled out the cork and, when nothing happened, peered inside. It seemed to be empty. She tried shaking it, then held it up to her ear. Still nothing.

Again she turned to Norman. He had his arms folded across his chest and was looking at her with raised eyebrows.

Jennifer rubbed the bottle.

Suddenly it grew warm in her hands and a whiff of smoke materialized. Jennifer dropped the bottle as the whiff turned to a pink puff; then the puff thickened into a red cloud. The cloud started to laugh. Before Jennifer had time to think, "That's odd!" a full-size jinni dressed in red and gold was standing before her.

He was very tall and stood with his hands on his wide hips, laughing heartily in a manner more jolly than frightening. He wore gold chains and armbands and earrings that jingled whenever he moved. His eyes were green, and—although Jennifer and Norman didn't know it—they were the exact color of the sea by the house he had left long ago. And like the sea at noon, they sparkled brightly.

"Oh!" Jennifer exclaimed, as he made a sweeping bow to her. She wasn't sure what the proper greeting for a jinni was, so she just silently curtsied and looked him over carefully.

The jinni turned to Norman and bowed again. "I am the jinni of the bottle," he said. (No accent, Jennifer noted.) "I understand you are my new master."

"The two of us," Norman corrected.

"Ah, a partnership! Are you aware that there are rules?"

"Yes, but we don't know what they are."

"Ah!" the jinni said again. "Actually, there are only two. First, you get one wish."

Jennifer nodded eagerly and the jinni smiled encouragingly.

"And the second rule simply defines the limitations on what that wish can be."

"Sounds fair," Norman grudgingly agreed. "How many limitations are there?"

"Nine hundred and eighty-three," the jinni answered, gesturing and pulling a leather-bound book from the air.

Jennifer's eyes grew large.

"I'll just go over the main points," the jinni assured them. "I can be summoned back any number of times for clarification."

"What have we gotten ourselves into?" Norman sighed.

The jinni smiled reassuringly and put on a pair of wire-rimmed glasses. Then he tapped one of his jeweled fingers on the first page. "Now, I said you get one wish, and that means one. You can't wish for more wishes; you can't wish for another jinni; you can't wish for magic power."

Norman nodded, and the jinni skipped ahead at least a hundred pages.

"You can't wish to destroy any magic object belonging to someone else, and you can't break a spell somebody else has cast."

Norman exhaled loudly and glanced at Jennifer.

The jinni looked over his rimmed glasses in time to see their expressions. "Ah," he said thoughtfully.

He ran his finger down several pages before stopping again. "You're not allowed to tamper with the nature of the world. That includes going back to yesterday or extending today, changing the order of the seasons, turning the moon to green cheese, that sort of thing.

"Further, I'm not allowed to harm anyone for you, and I can't force people to do something they don't want to do."

The jinni turned some more pages. "Your wish can't be too general, like for 'happiness' or 'peace.' You have to ask for something specific. 'A bottomless pot of gold' is very popular," he suggested hopefully, and looked up to see what reaction this got.

When it didn't get any, he flipped through the last pages with a gentle tinkling of armbands and chains. "Almost through. Ah, yes. I can't advise you directly or give you any information or insights."

The jinni closed the book and folded it into the air in front of him. "Any questions?"

Norman raised his eyebrows. "What good are you?"

"Ah, well," the jinni said noncommittally, removing his glasses and putting them away with his book.

"You said you can't break someone else's spell," Jennifer said. "But Norman looks old because of his *own* spell. Can you make him young again?"

"Assuredly."

Norman held up his hand. "Maybe later," he told Jennifer, "if we don't need him for something more important."

Jennifer thought being stuck looking like someone's great-grandfather was pretty important, but Norman had already turned back to the jinni. "Is there a time limit to this wish?"

"You may take as long as you need to make up your minds."

"And afterward," Jennifer asked, "what about you?"

"Your decision entirely. Most often I am, ahm—how can I put this delicately?—traded for something of value."

This reminded them of Norman's lost ring and didn't really answer her question. "But how long do you have to remain in the bottle?" she asked.

"A BOTTOMLESS POT OF GOLD IS VERY POPULAR", HE SUGGESTED HOPEFULLY.

"Ah!" the jinni said. "You mean, 'When is a jinni not a jinni?' "

She nodded.

For a second it seemed as if he didn't plan to answer, but he was only remembering a happy life hastily traded long ago for an endless one. And once again his mind saw the little house by the boundless sea. "Never, I'm afraid," he answered. "There can't be a magic bottle without a jinni."

He shrugged away an angry memory. "Worse things could have happened." He made a vague gesture and his bracelets clinked softly. "Are you ready to make your wish?"

"No," Norman decided. "We'll save it for when we really need it."

The jinni bowed and was gone, leaving only a pinkish haze that settled to the ground with the faintest jingling.

"Oh, my," Jennifer said.

"Indeed," Norman agreed.

A Second Plan

If Jennifer had found Norman's first plan to be a bit vague and shaky (and to be perfectly honest, she did), that was nothing compared to what she thought of his next plan.

To get the jinni from the Old Witch and just see what happened from there was haphazard enough, but she couldn't believe she had heard correctly when he told her his new idea.

"Excuse me, but I think there's something wrong with my ears," Jennifer said, tapping one of them. "I thought you said, 'We're going to try to find Malveenya herself.'"

"Forget your ears," Norman said. "There's nothing else we can do."

Obviously methodical planning was not one of Norman's strong points. But in this case he was right—they faced the choice of forgetting about Alexander or of confronting Malveenya. And when she thought back to Alexander's arrogant, selfish ways, Jennifer had to admit to herself that the idea of letting sleeping princes lie was very appealing.

But she knew she couldn't do that, and she realized she couldn't come up with any plan better than Norman's, so she had to agree.

"Should we get some help from my father's army?" Jennifer asked. She was afraid to think how worried the old king would be by now, and drew a mental picture of him sending out the troops to look for her. Unfortunately, the kingdom had been at peace for so long that there was no full-time army, only the reserves who met for parades and grand openings and such.

Jennifer recalled the last time she had seen them in action. "Parade, march!" the sergeant at arms had called so loudly that a boy who normally worked on his father's farm dropped his rusty shield, which tripped the part-time basket weaver carrying King Frederick's standard, which bopped the head of the stable hand in front of him who wasn't wearing his helmet because he was busy trying to fix its leather chin strap. The stable hand immediately gave a terrific yell, which caused two-thirds of the army to drop shields and swords and jump into the bushes. The men remaining weren't necessarily the bravest but they were wearing ill-fitted helmets that pressed against their ears and prevented them from hearing anything. So they stood milling about saying, "Whazzat? What happened?" Her father's army would hardly—Jennifer admitted to herself—be a decided advantage.

"We could go back and get them to help us," Norman was saying, "but this is probably a situation where we need quickness and cleverness rather than brute force."

The army certainly didn't have brute force, and considering the alternative qualities Norman had named, Jennifer decided to forget the subject entirely. "What exactly are we going to do?" she asked.

"I thought we'd just find Malveenya and see what happens from there."

Jennifer didn't mention that this was what she'd been afraid he would say, but asked instead how they'd find Malveenya.

He explained that her main home was in a place called the Valley of Darkness and Despair. Norman knew the general direction, but warned that the forest road sometimes seemed to have a mind of its own— which was something Jennifer had begun to suspect the day before.

"Right, then," she said, with what she hoped was a determined and ready-for-anything expression, "we're off."

So, with Jennifer carrying the magic bottle in one of the huge pockets in her gown, the two of them set out hand-in-hand to find the most powerful evil creature in the forest.

The forest road ended.

One minute it was twisting and turning in its usual infuriating way; the next it was abruptly gone. The bricks led to a thick wall of trees, then stopped. There wasn't the faintest indication of a dirt path or a chipmunk trail or even a spider track (although Jennifer had to take Norman's word for this last one). Dead end. Nothing. Nowhere to go.

"What now?" Jennifer asked.

The sorcerer, who had been even quieter and more withdrawn than usual for the last hour, didn't answer immediately. He studied the angle of the sun and tried to see how far the thick growth of trees that faced them stretched on either side.

"If my bearings are correct," he finally said, "this is it."

"The Valley of Darkness and Despair?"

Norman nodded.

"Where do we get in?" Jennifer's voice was faint because she still wasn't exactly sure she wanted to get in at all.

Norman tugged on his beard a bit. "My first guess would be right here. I know it doesn't look very likely, but I think it doesn't look any more likely anywhere else."

Jennifer remembered what Norman had said about the road having a mind of its own. "It seems to have led us here," she said. "Doesn't it?"

"Yes," he said. With that, he pushed aside a branch and stepped through the row of trees that marked the edge of the Valley of Darkness and Despair.

In the Valley of
Darkness and Despair

A regular path never reappeared, but the position of the bushes, trees, and undergrowth didn't allow them to make any decisions about which way to go. In a sense this was an advantage, since the trees blocked out the sun and they quickly lost all feeling of north, south, east, and west. The only directions they could be sure of were up and down. And it was soon obvious that wherever they were going, it was gradually, but unchangingly, downhill.

Jennifer was just beginning to wonder if there was no more to life than lifting one foot after the other over thick tree roots and squeezing between the clinging branches of tall, scrubby-looking bushes when, suddenly, she realized that the trees up ahead had a different light to them.

Norman had noticed, too, but there was no need to say anything, for this seemed to be where the forest was leading them.

A second later Jennifer saw that the new light was coming from a clearing.

She reached into her pocket to touch the magic bottle and quietly followed Norman out of the shadow of the trees.

Before them was a thatched-roof house that took up most of the clearing.

As soon as her mind registered this, Jennifer corrected herself. Something was out of scale; the perspective was all wrong. She closed her eyes, counted to five, and looked again.

The house was not right there before them; it was still some distance away. And the clearing was enormous; it just looked small because the house took up so much of it.

The chimney reached as high as the trees, and the windows were almost as tall and wide as Norman's whole cottage. Each post of the white fence around the house was made from a hefty tree trunk pounded into the ground. There was a cobblestone walk starting where they stood and going to the front door, but it was much wider than the main road in Jennifer's village and it ended in a step that was almost as tall as she was.

"Oh-oh," Norman said.

Jennifer couldn't have put it better. She was about to take a step back into the cover of the trees when a rough, dry voice bellowed, "Hey!"

The two of them turned around and found themselves staring at the top laces of someone's boot.

Jennifer tilted her head, and leaned back, and looked up, up—till she reached the man's face, almost ten times as high up as where she would have found it on an average man.

Now giants have never been known for their beauty. Even to other giants, they aren't very appealing. But this giant was especially ugly. He had longish, straggly hair that left greasy stains on his collar, and his huge belly strained at the belt, from which hung a ten-foot-long hunting knife. In shape, color, and texture the giant's nose resembled a moldy potato; even his ears had warts.

He leaned way down to place his face close to theirs and tapped a finger with a cracked yellow nail on Norman's chest. "What," he demanded, "do ya think yer doing here?"

The sorcerer met his red-veined eyes without flinching, though the giant's "tap" had almost knocked him over. "Just passing through," he explained.

"Well, ya can't."

"Okay," Norman agreed readily, more than willing at this point to forget everything and go back home.

"Not so fast," the giant said. "Here youse are trespassing on my land, just traipsing through without a by-yer-leave, or an apology, or nothing."

"Sorry," Norman said.

Jennifer nodded to show she was sorry, too.

"Sorry don't pay the taxes. Now that yer already here, I gotta charge ya the toll."

Norman and Jennifer exchanged a worried look. "We don't have any money."

The giant shook his huge head in disgust. "People!" he muttered. "Always trying to get away with something. All right, I'll tell ya what I'm gonna do." The dirty finger found Norman's chest again. "I'll let *you* go and get the money if ya leave the girl behind as security."

Jennifer gulped.

Without hesitation, Norman said, politely, "No, I don't think so."

"Then it's into the supper pot with both of youse," the giant said, and tucked each of them under a hairy arm.

He carried them into his house and put them in a huge pot on the kitchen table while he got the fire burning brightly.

Jennifer started to pull the magic bottle out of her pocket, but Norman shook his head. "We'd better save that in case we need it later," he whispered.

"I don't know much about these things, but just as a guess I'd say we need it now." Jennifer whispered also, but the giant was whistling to himself as he peeled watermelon-size potatoes, so he couldn't hear them anyway.

"No, not really," Norman said, raising his voice considerably and standing on tiptoe to see over the edge of the pot. "Giants are very stupid, you know."

Somehow this didn't seem the right thing to say, considering the circumstances, and Jennifer put her finger to her lips even though the giant gave no indication that he had heard.

"No, really," Norman insisted even more loudly. "There are a lot of stupid creatures in the world, but none more stupid than a giant."

"Eh?" the giant asked, as Jennifer made frantic shushing motions. "Were youse guys talking to me?"

"I was talking to Jennifer," Norman explained.

"Oh." The giant started to turn back.

"I was telling her how incredibly slow giants are." Jennifer groaned.

"Slow?" the giant said. "How do ya mean, slow?"

"Dull. Stupid. You know, slow."

"Not to start an argument or nothing," the giant said, his feelings somewhat bruised, "but yer the ones in the soup kettle."

This was a good point, but Norman ignored it. "Exactly." He turned to Jennifer and said, louder than necessary, "Would you look at that? He's peeling potatoes and carrots. Giants have no sense of class. Do you know what the head waiter in a fancy restaurant says when he sees a giant coming?"

Jennifer shook her head.

"He says, 'Bring out the leftovers. Get the wilted lettuce and the day-old bread. This one's too stupid to know the difference.' "

"Is that what he says?" Jennifer asked, although her heart wasn't in it.

Norman nodded somberly. "Giants are a laughing-stock. Nobody takes them seriously. Potatoes and carrots, indeed!"

The giant came over and pulled the two of them out of the pot. He set them on the table where he could see them better. "What's wrong with potatoes and carrots?"

"Well, if I have to be somebody's dinner," Norman said, "I should hope it would be in a meal with a little more sophistication than pot-luck stew."

The giant wasn't really all that bad a fellow, and he didn't want to hurt Norman's pride, so he explained, "But I like stew."

"You like stew," Norman repeated. He turned to Jennifer. "There you have it. Potatoes and carrots. Well, it's his upbringing, I imagine. He can't help it. I suppose he doesn't know any better."

The giant couldn't understand what all the fuss was about, so he just shrugged and started to turn back to his preparations.

"The least you could do," Norman said hurriedly, before he lost the giant's attention completely, "is add some"—he tried to think of something with the sound of fancy gourmet cooking—"some chopped essence of crème-de-menthe parfait."

Of course, there was no such thing in those days any more than there is today. It's something the great chefs of the world have simply never bothered to invent, but it was the best he could come up with on the spur of the moment.

Jennifer gave him a startled look, but said nothing.

The giant had no idea what Norman was talking about, but he certainly wasn't going to admit that.

Norman broke the silence. "Haven't you ever heard of . . . ? No, of course not. Sorry I brought it up." He smiled sweetly.

The nature of giants being what it is, he answered indignantly, "Of course I heard of it. It's, uh, chopped. And it's, ahm . . ." He couldn't remember any of the other words Norman had used. "It's for cooking. Comes in a little box." He figured this description was probably general enough to fit just about anything and hoped it would convince these two that he wasn't all that dumb.

Indeed, the old man was looking impressed. "I'm surprised you've heard of it." He gave another sweet smile. "I don't suppose you've ever actually tried any."

"Oh, yeah, sure," the giant said, determined not to let Norman get the upper hand. "I eat it all the time. Never start a meal without it."

Norman nodded as if he approved, then said, "Well?"

The giant considered. "Oh," he said. "Ahmmm." Then he snapped his fingers as if disappointed. "Wouldn't ya know—I just ran out of my last box of it this morning."

Norman turned to Jennifer with a triumphant cry. "There! See! What did I tell you? Giants try to act as if they've got class, but inside they're all the same."

"Sorry," the giant said. Even if he was about to eat these people, he didn't want them thinking badly of him. "I woulda gotten some more, but, ahm, I didn't know where to get any this time of year."

"Oh," Norman said. "This season? Barcelona."

"Barcelona?" the giant croaked.

"You have heard of Barcelona?"

"Well, yeah, but the distance . . ."

"For a giant of your size?" Norman said. "A hop, skip, and a jump away. You'll be there and back in no time."

Every giant likes to think of himself as being the biggest and the best, and this one was no exception,

so he didn't really want to argue the point. "I dunno," he started doubtfully.

"The other giants'll be green with envy."

The giant scratched his head and wondered how he had gotten into this. "Barcelona, huh?"

Norman nodded. "And that will be just long enough for us to take a nap before supper." He gave a great yawn as he sat down on the table with his back resting on the kettle. "We've been traveling all day, and we're very tired."

When Jennifer continued to stand there, just looking at him, he glared at her and repeated, more slowly, "*Very* tired."

"What?" Jennifer said in a slow, lazy voice. "I'm sorry, I'm so tired I wasn't listening." She stretched and yawned, then slowly sank down beside Norman.

The giant rubbed the stubble on his face and fought back a yawn of his own. "You'll show me how to cook this?" he asked, putting on his coat.

With his eyes closed, Norman nodded. Jennifer sat very quietly by his side and worked on looking sleepy and helpless.

"I really appreciate this," the giant called from the door.

"No problem," Norman assured him. "Believe me, it's my pleasure."

He remained very still until the giant's heavy footsteps could no longer be heard, then he sprang to his feet and ran to the edge of the fifty-foot-long table.

"It's sort of high, but not too bad," he told Jennifer, pointing to the chair that was pulled up nearby.

They jumped from the table to the chair, and then climbed down the chair leg. The giant had made the furniture himself, and since he wasn't a very careful craftsman, the chair leg wasn't sanded down smoothly; there were plenty of ridges to give Jennifer and Norman firm footholds to make their descent easier.

Once on the floor, they began moving the chair toward the door. This involved quite a bit of pulling, pushing, tugging, and dragging, but finally they had it where they wanted it. They rested only long enough to get their breaths back, all the while hoping that the giant wouldn't change his mind or decide that he needed his galoshes or anything like that.

Norman scampered back up the chair (tripping over his feet several times until he divided his beard in two and tied it around his neck like a woolly scarf so that he could see). From there he was able to reach the doorknob, and after considerable strain, he managed to turn the dartboard-size knob with both hands.

Jennifer, pushing against the door, felt it give, and she fell headlong into the backyard.

Then Norman was by her side and the two of them made a dash for the trees, hoping that once they got back into the cover of the forest the giant would never be able to find them.

All the while they ran, Norman kept calculating: If the giant spotted them *now* and started chasing them at this very instant, could they make it to the distant trees before he reached them? How about now?

Jennifer kept one hand pressed against her aching side and the other in her pocket, clutching the magic bottle, and wondered—since their progress seemed so slow—if they were running without moving, the way it happens in dreams.

Finally they were there—among the safety of the trees, and still there was no sign of the giant. The two of them ran several steps more before tumbling, exhausted, to the ground.

Still in the Valley of Darkness and Despair

They still couldn't see the sky, but they could tell from the increasing dimness that night had almost caught up with them.

Around them they could hear the underbrush crackle with the movements of unseen creatures. Sometimes, out of the corner of an eye, one of them would spot a dark streak jumping for cover as they passed. Birds were bringing the last meal of the evening to their chicks. All the small animals who scamper about in the sunlight were settling down for a comfortable sleep in their nests or burrows. The night predators were getting ready to prowl.

The two travelers had heard no sound of pursuit from the giant and were just beginning to congratulate themselves on their elusiveness when a silky voice hissed, "What's this? Escaped from the giant's premises, I perceive."

And there in front of them, where two seconds before there had been nothing, now stood a very large dragon.

The only time Jennifer had ever seen a dragon before was that morning when the Old Witch had made herself look like one. That had been frightening enough, even when she had known it was only an illusion. Now she stood stunned, only her hand moving, groping for her pocket, fingering the magic bottle.

Norman's hand was on her wrist. "We might need it more later," he whispered.

"You know I'm new to all this," Jennifer answered just as quietly, "but I don't see how we could ever need it more than now."

"Please," the dragon said, "no whispering." He smiled, showing many long, pointed teeth, then added, "It distresses me." He demonstrated what happened when he became distressed with a blast of flame that shriveled the grass at their feet.

They took a quick step backward and the dragon took two forward. He moved his enormous tail back and forth, knocking several branches off trees.

Now dragons, as any zoologist will tell you, are closely related to snakes, which explains the hissing manner of their speech. But a more important trait that the two share is the way they can fix their eyes on a creature as if looking into the farthest corners of its being and almost hypnotize that victim into not moving until it's too late to escape. Which is precisely what this particular dragon was doing at that very moment. His eyes were like black whirlpools, and he slowly approached, whispering, "So, small strangers, you've absconded from the savage giant's sagging domicile?"

Norman managed to break eye contact, and the dragon momentarily stopped advancing.

The sorcerer was visibly shaken and he stalled for time. "We didn't exactly abscond," he said. "The giant sneaked out first."

"And will you say why the giant should need to sneak from his own house?"

"No," Norman said.

"No?" the dragon repeated. "No?"

"I know what you're planning. You want me to talk so I'll be distracted, and then you'll jump us."

"I wouldn't think of such a thing," said the dragon, who was thinking exactly that.

"You won't even be listening to what I'm saying."

"I assure you, I'll be savoring every single syllable."

Having just escaped from one supper pot, Norman didn't care for the way the dragon said "savoring," but noted with professional interest that the dragon's snake-long tongue and his tendency to stress his S's made for an interesting combination. The dragon's tongue flicked and curled around itself with each S-word he uttered. Norman wondered if it was physically possible for the dragon's tongue to tie itself into a knot. *That* would surely keep him and Jennifer from getting singed . . . or worse.

Hoping to keep the dragon's mind off eating them, and at the same time to keep himself from succumbing to the dragon's hypnotic power, Norman said, "Well, you see, the giant was making some swill— stew, actually."

"I've sampled it. Swill is closer."

"Substandard stuff?" Norman asked.

"Substandard swilly stew. Go on."

"Well, we just suggested some spices for it. Are you sure you're really paying attention?"

The dragon nodded to encourage him. "You suggested several spices for some substandard swilly stew. Yes?"

"Essential ones for sweetening it."

"You suggested several essential spices to sweeten some substandard swilly stew. So what?"

"The giant didn't have them, so he sneaked away to the sandy Spanish seashore to steal some."

The dragon nodded. "Let me see if I've got this straight," he said to prove that he really was listening. "The shameless giant simply sneaked from his own house to the sandy Spanish seashore especially to steal several essential spices to sweeten some substandard swilly stew?" His long tongue leapt, curled, and curved.

"Right. While he was away, we slipped silently through his snare."

"Sly," the dragon had to admit.

"Well, if he wasn't so self-seeking, it never would have happened. And as it was, we had to act swiftly. Are you following all this?"

"That shameless, self-seeking giant let swift, sly strangers slip silently through his snare just so he could sneak to the sandy Spanish seashore especially to steal several essential spices to sweeten some substandard swilly stew!" The dragon's tongue danced, its tip touching its middle before it slid down and straightened while Norman tried not to show any interest.

"That scalawag possesses the scruples of celery," the sorcerer continued.

"A single stalk," Jennifer offered, seeing at last what Norman was up to.

Norman fumbled with his beard so the dragon wouldn't catch him smiling.

"And a soggy one at that," she added.

Norman nodded. "He slackened his senses sufficiently so that we could get away with it."

The dragon sighed. "So, that shameless, self-seeking scalawag, possessing scarcely the scruples of a single, soggy stalk of celery, has slackened his senses sufficiently so that swift, sly strangers could slip silently through his snare just so he could sneak to the sandy Spanish seashore especially to steal several essential spices to sweeten some substandard swilly stew." The dragon's tongue was just a pink flash as it spun and waved and corkscrewed and untwisted.

"Sad isn't it?" Norman asked.

"Sad that the shameless—" The dragon abruptly choked on his tongue, which was still whipping about a bit from his last mouthful. "Grawarrr!" he bellowed. A tongue of flame burst from his mouth and nearly singed Norman's whiskers.

The sorcerer took a quick step back.

"Enough of these silly games already!" the dragon roared. "I see what you're trying to do, you sad little sample of humanity! Well, it got you about two extra minutes and that's all. You'll find I'm not so stupid as that slobbering giant!"

"Sir," Norman said in a voice of injured innocence, "I was only describing the circumstances. Everyone knows that the youngest, most immature dragon is by far smarter than the most scholarly giant."

The dragon smoothed down his scales. "Well, it's very nice of you to say so, but I'm going to eat you anyway."

Norman tried his best to ignore this last comment and think up some other tactic. "I only brought it up for your benefit."

The dragon's eyes narrowed suspiciously. "Still speaking in circles, I discern. What are you talking about?"

"Gold."

"Gold?" Now the dragon's eyes opened wide and glowed even more brightly than before. For while it may be debatable whether, as a class, giants or dragons are more stubbornly proud, there can be no doubt in the world which one is the most greedy creature ever to draw breath. And luckily Norman had finally remembered this. "Gold," the dragon repeated. He pursed his lips and let some steam blow out his ears. "Ah, gold. In the giant's house? You saw it? Where?"

Norman almost froze. "Have you ever heard of a giant without a hoard of gold?"

"No, but I've been there. I've never seen—"

"Well, he wouldn't keep piles of it on the kitchen table, knowing you could snatch it away with your superior strength and intellect."

"Snatch the smirky fellow's gold," the dragon hissed to himself.

"SNATCH THE SMIRKY FELLOW'S GOLD," THE DRAGON HISSED TO HIMSELF.

"While he's away in Spain."

This was a mistake. The dragon's eyes abruptly refocused on them, and he snapped warily, "Stealing several essential spices to sweeten some substandard swilly stew?"

"I only mentioned it to show there's time. But not much."

"I must dispose of you first."

"It's *your* gold slipping through *your* fingers."

It wasn't his gold yet, and claws would have been more accurate than fingers, but the dragon got the point anyway. "Grawarrr!" he cried again, for he hated decisions. But meals were easier to come by than gold, so in another moment he had brushed them aside.

For the next few seconds, they could hear him barging through the trees in the direction of the giant's home. Then they were all alone in the quiet dark of Malveenya's valley.

Nighttime

Only a little bit of moonlight was able to filter through the thickness of the trees. Jennifer and Norman could barely make out the way and held hands so they wouldn't become separated as they slowly fought their way forward.

The breaking of any twig in the darkness behind them, the whisper of any creature gliding through the grass made their bodies cringe in expectation of an angry bellow from the giant or a burst of steam and fire from the dragon. Jennifer thought briefly about how fond she was becoming of Norman and how— despite his lack of real magical ability—he made her feel more safe and comfortable than she had any right to feel, given their present circumstances.

Partially to cover up some of the night's noises, and also to lift each other's spirits, they once again tried to piece together the magic mirror's riddle. "Lesson One: Don't disbelieve something just because you can't see it." And, "Lesson Two: If the answer isn't in you, it isn't." But still they got nowhere. Even when Jennifer remembered the mirror saying, "A kiss usually works, but not always," they couldn't come up with anything.

Besides, ever since talking with the dragon, Norman kept speaking in *S*'s, and it was beginning to drive Jennifer crazy.

They had put aside for the moment the problem of the mirror and were trying to catch glimpses of the stars through the branches, when Jennifer said, "There's one. No, wait. That's too low to be a star."

"Strange," Norman murmured.

They walked a few more steps, then Jennifer saw another light that looked like a star but wasn't. Another moment and Norman had spotted several more. "Candles?" he asked, as if he didn't dare to hope.

As they made their hesitant way forward, the trees thinned and the two travelers were standing in a wide clearing before a magnificent palace.

Unlike most castles of those days, which were built to be used as forts able to protect townspeople in times of siege, this one seemed to be purely a decorative home. Built of white stone that gleamed in the moonlight, it had spires and peaks and turrets reaching airily toward the sky. Everywhere there were large windows with balconies, and in each one they could see a glowing candle.

They became aware of the soft sound of a flute playing, and this mixed pleasantly with the gurgling of the brook that circled the majestic palace. It wasn't much of a moat, for at its deepest point it wouldn't have reached their knees; but in any case, the drawbridge was down.

"Maybe whoever lives here can help us," Jennifer hoped out loud.

"Maybe," Norman answered.

They stepped on a path of brightly colored, crushed stones that was lit by little round jars of burning oil. On either side of them were elaborate garden beds whose sweet smell came only faintly, since the flowers were closed for the night.

Standing in the dark on the forest side of the drawbridge, they could make out little of the palace's entry hall.

"Hello," Norman called out. The flute-playing continued and there was no answer. "Hello," he called more loudly, with Jennifer adding her voice this time.

When the music continued uninterrupted, they cautiously crossed the bridge and stepped into the main hall. If the giant had circled around and gotten there first, Jennifer still would not have been able to move. If the dragon had been standing just inside the door with black smoke billowing from his nostrils and flames leaping from his mouth, Norman would not have noticed. If Malveenya herself had been waiting for them, it still wouldn't have made any difference. They would have reacted in the same way. For the room they had entered was the most beautiful either of them had ever seen.

As it so happened, there was no one there, and they were able to stand in mute amazement simply absorbing their splendid surroundings.

The walls were white marble, lit by two enormous crystal chandeliers that hung in many glittering tiers.

The ceiling high above their heads was a huge mirror that seemed to stretch the entire width and length of the room without a seam. It was only when Jennifer stepped closer to the fountain in the center of the room that she saw a large circular hole had been cut, and a huge glass dome showed the star-sprinkled heavens.

Besides the soothing sounds of flute and water, Norman heard the light chirping of a bird. At first he thought his imagination was affected by all the plants and potted fruit trees growing everywhere in the room, but then he noticed a hanging cage almost as big as his entire cottage. He stepped nearer and saw an exotically colored bird such as he had never seen before.

With Norman studying the bird and Jennifer fascinated by the skylight, neither heard the soft step on the landing above the stairs.

"Greetings, travelers," a gentle, melodious voice called. "And welcome to my home."

Norman and Jennifer turned to face the beautiful woman who had spoken. She had thick golden hair that almost reached the floor. Her large blue eyes sparkled merrily in a face with a perfect pink complexion. She smiled warmly and made a sweeping motion with her slim hand, saying, "Everything you see is yours to share."

She came down the curving staircase and walked toward them with the graceful movement of an ice skater. Jennifer started to curtsy, but the tall, slender woman stopped her with a gentle hand on her arm.

"There's no need for formality," she said in the same quiet voice. "We're all friends here." The silk sleeve of her shimmering white gown brushed against Jennifer and it felt as cool and smooth as running water. It reminded Jennifer that her own simple gown had become dirty and tattered around the edges, and she guessed that her face was probably smudged.

Suddenly the woman's brow creased in concern. "But my poor dears," she murmured, "you look exhausted! Come, let me get you some food and drink and prepare a place for you to rest."

Jennifer glanced at Norman, who was standing quite still, and she wondered if the sorcerer was being quiet out of shyness or if he had forgotten that he no longer had the magic ring and thought he had changed himself to look like an inconspicuous coat rack. In any case, all the questions that needed asking seemed left to her. "But where are we?" she asked in a voice that she felt sounded childishly high-pitched and ugly compared to the other's.

The beautiful woman smiled cheerfully. "Why, you're in my home. And this is as warm and safe a place as you'll find around here."

"But I thought we were in the Valley of Darkness and Despair," Norman said when it became obvious that she wasn't about to clarify this answer.

The woman started to laugh merrily, but quickly forced herself to stop. "I'm sorry. I didn't mean to be rude," she said, her eyes twinkling. "But does this look like the Valley of Darkness and Despair?"

She pulled two apples from one of the small trees and offered one to each of them. "Why don't you have an apple," she suggested, "and I'll see about getting something more substantial for you to eat from the kitchen. Do make yourselves at home."

She smiled encouragingly and left.

"My goodness!" Jennifer said when they were alone.

"How in the world could we have wandered out of the valley?" Norman asked. He placed his apple on the windowsill and thoughtfully stared out into the clear night.

Jennifer sat on the circular bench surrounding the fountain. She was very hungry, but Norman's sudden moodiness in the face of their obvious good luck disturbed her. Besides, something kept nagging at the edges of her mind.

She twirled her apple on the edge of the fountain in time to the melody the flute was still playing. Something someone had said. Norman? Alexander? No, it was the Old Witch. "Something about apples," Jennifer thought. "Or was it eating in general?"

She shrugged and picked up the fruit. But it was still wobbling from the last spin she had given it; it slipped through her fingers and into the fountain.

There was a loud hiss as the water bubbled and steamed. Norman turned to face Jennifer as she jumped to her feet. "Norman!" she gasped. "What happened? What does this mean?"

"It means," came the cool, level voice of their beautiful hostess from the doorway, where she had reentered, "that Lesson Three is: Don't believe everything you see."

"Lesson Three?" Jennifer said, looking at her blankly.

Then both she and Norman, at the same instant, whispered, "Malveenya!"

The flute music changed into the shrieking of the wind, which suddenly blew around the palace and through the room. As Norman ran to Jennifer's side, the room darkened as white marble turned to black stone and crystal chandeliers became heavy wrought-iron lamps. The mirrored ceiling was lost in flickering shadows caused by the jagged flashes of lightning that struck but did not break the skylight.

Jennifer twisted her face away from the stinging strands of hair that the wind blew into her eyes, and saw the flowers and fruit trees wither into dark, stunted scrub brush with burrs and poisonous-looking berries.

Malveenya stood with the wind whipping her golden hair behind her. Beautiful but terrible, she added her harsh laugh to the frantic cawing of the now-black buzzard, screaming in its cramped cage.

"Greetings, travelers," she repeated. "And welcome to my home."

Malveenya

Malveenya took a step toward the two young people who huddled together. If anything, she was more beautiful than when they had first seen her. Her eyes blazed, her cheeks were flushed, her brilliant white teeth showed in an evil smile.

"So," she smirked, "you were able to outsmart a giant and a dragon. That doesn't automatically qualify you for any awards for cleverness, you know." Although lightning still lit the room irregularly, the wind had died down and she was able to speak without raising her voice.

She stepped closer and examined Jennifer coolly. "All day," she said. "All day to get here! What a slow and dreary child in every respect!"

She turned her attention to Norman. "And you, you silly old goat, where ever did she pick you up? I'm so disappointed! I have visitors so infrequently and I was truly hoping you'd be interesting. Kreech, stop that noise this instant!"

This last statement was directed at the dark-eyed buzzard who was furiously banging against his cage to the constant high-pitched screaming of a sound very similar to his name. The bird grabbed one of the bars with his hooked beak and gave the cage one last angry rattle before settling down to smooth his plumage. Then he began a lesser series of grumbling noises.

In the instant Malveenya turned her attention away, Jennifer's hand found her pocket. "Now, Norman," she thought. "If ever, now." But already it was too late. The older woman was again watching her, her blue eyes looking like a winter storm that comes howling down the mountain to overtake the unsuspecting climber— cold, brutal, relentless.

Malveenya was trying to stare her down. If Jennifer had realized this, she would have looked away immediately, but her mind was elsewhere. Things said and things unsaid were beginning to come together. "She doesn't know," Jennifer realized. "She doesn't know that Norman isn't really old and she doesn't know about the jinni in the bottle. She isn't all-powerful. She might be able to see into the cottage because of the magic mirror, and she might know what goes on inside this valley, but she isn't all-powerful." Jennifer repeated this last part several times, as if it were a charm, and removed her hand from the magic bottle. Then she looked away from Malveenya.

"Do you love Prince Alexander?" Malveenya purred.

Love wasn't the right word—Jennifer *cared* about what happened to the prince, but she wasn't *in love* with him. But it was too much to explain, so she nodded, without looking up. She felt Norman shift position next to her.

"And do you care for this old man, this Norman?"

Malveenya had gotten it backward—Jennifer suddenly realized she *loved* Norman—but again she just nodded. She could sense the sorcerer staring at her, but didn't look up until Malveenya asked, "Will you do something for me?"

The enchantress circled the two young people. "I have great power," she said. "But I want more. Years ago, the magic wall was built to limit me. If I stay on this side of the wall, I can do anything I want; if I cross to the other side, I have no powers."

This didn't seem like a problem. "So stay here," Jennifer suggested.

"No!" Malveenya cried. "What use is limitless power in this place? I want to live in the outside world!"

"But if you can't pass through the gate without losing your power—"

"Ah! But there's where you come in."

That's what Jennifer had been afraid of.

Malveenya continued. "Magic cannot destroy the wall. But ordinary people—working with picks and shovels and hammers—can. I want you to return to your home and convince the people that the wall is a nuisance. Tell them that the forest is a beautiful park that everyone should enjoy. Tell them there are gigantic trees on which money grows. Tell them anything, but get them to tear down that wall so I can leave!"

"No!" Jennifer gasped. She couldn't begin to guess what Malveenya planned to do if she were free to roam, but judging from the state of things in the Valley of Darkness and Despair, it didn't seem a good idea. "I couldn't."

Malveenya smiled cheerfully. "Do you love Prince Alexander?" she asked again. "Do you love Norman? What if something terrible happened to them? Have a good night's sleep while you think about it."

She glided to the cage from which the buzzard, Kreech, glared at her suspiciously with half-lowered eyelids. He took a quick step back and resumed his terrible cries as the enchantress opened the door. But when she pulled back her billowing sleeve and stuck her arm in the cage, he obediently and gently stepped onto her arm and let himself be pulled out.

Her eyes never wavering from Jennifer and Norman, Malveenya set the buzzard on the floor, then took a step back.

Immediately the large bird began to grow larger. He beat his short, broad wings helplessly as his body became taller and wider and his feathers turned to flapping black cloth. The shape of his face changed slightly and in no time at all they stood facing a man. Admittedly, he still had the look of a bird of prey—the constantly moving eyes were fierce and piercing, the nose was sharp and beaklike, and the hands looked like talons. But he was still a man.

This was no illusion, Jennifer and Norman realized, no trick caused by a magic ring. Kreech had really been changed into a fearsome human.

Obviously this sort of thing had happened to Kreech before, and obviously he didn't like it at all. He stood for several seconds twitching his wingless shoulders and shifting his weight from one foot to the other; then he threw back his head and gave a wild screech. This was part declaration of freedom, part defiance, but mostly it was for show because he knew that—although out of the cage—he wasn't really free and that Malveenya—if she decided to—could easily shake all the defiance out of him.

"Kreech, would you be good enough to show our guests to their quarters?" Malveenya said sweetly. "Private accommodations, of course." She never would have trusted Kreech out of her sight in his bird form, but knew that he wouldn't try to escape now. Freedom to him didn't include being earthbound; it meant the ability to fly and soar and dive with his own kind.

Norman glanced at the sword Kreech wore at his side. "How good a swordsman could a bird possibly be?" he wondered, but decided he wan't really that curious.

Kreech stepped between the two prisoners and gripped Norman's left arm and Jennifer's right with strong, clawlike hands.

They started toward a narrow, dimly lit hall that wound steeply downward, and Norman mentally kicked himself for not having shifted places with Jennifer before the buzzard-man grabbed them. She had the magic bottle in her right pocket, so even though they were now out of Malveenya's sight, she couldn't get it out.

The hall became even narrower and they both

hunched their shoulders, shuddering at the thought of brushing against the rough walls, coated with spider-webs.

Norman tried to slow down and face Kreech, but found himself pulled along at the same rapid pace. "Wait," he said. "I have something to say to you."

"Quiet!" the buzzard-man said. His voice sounded so much like a caw, it took Norman a few seconds to realize that Kreech had spoken a human word. That, at least, was encouraging.

"You're a prisoner, too," he said. "We can help each other."

"Can't," Kreech answered.

"Look," Norman said. "She keeps you in a cage and she turns you into anything she pleases. If we work together, we can beat her."

Kreech remained silent.

Norman twisted around to look into his captor's face. The dark eyes reflected the torch flames, but were dull and unresponsive. Kreech might have the body of a man, Norman decided, but the mind was still that of a buzzard. The sorcerer doubted he could say anything that would reach him. He glanced at Jennifer, making movements with his head in the general direction of her pocket.

"Sir, you're hurting my arm," she said.

Kreech didn't answer or loosen his grip.

"Could you hold a little less tightly, please?"

Still no answer.

"Or could you switch arms for a while?"

Jennifer looked hopelessly at Norman. At the speed

they were being forced down the hall, she didn't dare try to get at the bottle with her left hand for fear she'd drop it.

Norman tried again. "I'm a sorcerer, Kreech," he admitted. "If you let us go, I can turn you back into a bird and you'll be free." Actually, he knew that was way beyond his powers, but he was desperate to get Kreech's attention. Kreech wasn't listening.

They stopped in front of a thick wooden door with a tiny, barred window. Kreech dropped Norman's arm to pull it open, then he jerked his head inside.

"One second," Norman started.

Kreech gave a wordless scream of rage as his hand gripped the sorcerer and spun him around and into the cell. Then he slammed the door shut and pulled Jennifer down the hall.

After a long, silent walk they came to another door. Kreech pushed her into the small, windowless cell. She heard the loud click of the lock, then the rustling of his robes as he shook himself and started back the way he had come.

Jennifer didn't dare use the magic bottle on her own. After Kreech had been gone awhile, she started calling the sorcerer's name, but their cells were too far apart. Finally she sank to the floor. "Norman, Norman," she whispered. "Do you have a plan? Tell me what to do."

But, of course, there was no answer.

The Wish

Somehow Jennifer had fallen asleep. She woke up suddenly when Kreech flung open the door and jerked his head for her to follow.

She stood up and tried to drive the grogginess from her mind.

"Quick!" Kreech cawed, and before she could move toward his other side, he again had his long, talonlike fingers wrapped around her right arm.

They walked swiftly to where they had left Norman. Kreech again said, "Quick!" in his rasping voice.

Norman looked grim and tired and Jennifer hoped he had been able to form a plan, for she hadn't. But as soon as he started to say, "You can't give in," Kreech cried, "Quiet!" and gave each of them a rough shake. They walked in silence the rest of the way back up to the main entry hall.

Malveenya was waiting for them. "Good morning, good morning," she called in a pleasant voice. "I do hope your rooms were adequate. So few guests drop by these days."

She smiled brightly and circled the three of them.

"Are all the cobwebs gone from your little mind?" she asked Jennifer. "Are you in the mood for a little reunion?"

Jennifer had no feeling of movement, but she could suddenly see dim colors and shapes about her. In another second they were standing in the cottage where she and Alexander had spent the night.

In fact, there before them was the sprawled form of the prince just as she had left him.

Malveenya went over and sat daintily on his chest. She looked up in time to catch Norman twitching his beard and making a gesture with this head. The girl obviously had no idea what he was trying to say, but Malveenya became annoyed anyway.

"Enough of that," she warned. "Keep still or I'll turn you into something incredibly nasty."

"It doesn't matter," Jennifer said.

"What?" the other two said at the same time, although Norman's voice cracked a bit.

"I've made my decision. I can't set you loose on the other side of the wall. No matter what you do, I won't help you."

"I'm afraid you don't understand, my dear," Malveenya said. "How would you like both your friends asleep forever? Why, look at this!" She leaned over and made a brushing motion over Alexander. "Dusty already. How would you like to spend the rest of your life alone in this cottage? No one to talk to, nowhere to go, nothing to do. Just you, the cottage, and two snoring dust collectors for the rest of your life.

"Or how would you like me to make you older than

"HOW WOULD YOU LIKE BOTH OF YOUR FRIENDS ASLEEP · · FOREVER?"

Norman here? Dry bones that crackle when you walk, back that hurts when it's going to rain, white hair, yellow teeth—or maybe no teeth at all—what man do you think would love you then?

"I could turn you into a fish and hold you half an inch above the water you need to live. Or I could turn you into a hairy spider and squash you. Why, I could even turn you into a bat's shadow and send you home. Then you'd be flitting about the ceiling making sad little squeaking noises and none of your friends or family would even know it's you.

"This is just off the top of my head, you realize. If I set my mind to it for a while, I'm sure I could come up with something better."

"I'm sure you could," Jennifer said, somewhat shakily. "But if you can do horrible things to us, you could do them to the people on the other side of the wall, too, and I can't help you do that."

"I suppose I could try to bribe you," Malveenya said. "Make you good-looking or rich or something. But rewarding loyalty isn't anywhere near as much fun as punishing disloyalty. Is it, Kreech?"

Still holding them, the buzzard-man made a movement as if ruffling his feathers, and Malveenya laughed heartily. Belonging to anyone else, it would have been rich, easy laughter—the kind that's catching. But Malveenya always laughed alone.

While her attention seemed elsewhere, Norman put his arm behind his back and tried to reach around Kreech.

Malveenya jumped to her feet. "I already warned you

once!" she screamed. Lowering her voice, she said, "You can let them go now, Kreech." She motioned Jennifer to come closer.

"Turn around," she ordered. "Watch your precious Norman. I'm going to melt him down into a little slimy puddle."

"No!" Jennifer gasped. "You can't!"

"Little girl, don't presume you can take that tone with me. Yes, I can and I will, and once it's done, there's no way to undo it."

Before Jennifer could move, Malveenya started to raise her arm, but then stopped of her own accord. "No, wait," she said, and Jennifer breathed a sigh of relief.

Malveenya continued in a friendly voice. "Norman, would you mind moving a little bit to the side? I don't want you ruining the table."

Norman stared at her blankly for a second. Whatever his plan was, Jennifer realized, it couldn't work if she didn't know it. She'd have to rely on herself.

Malveenya was still trying to gesture him away from the table when, in one movement, Jennifer rubbed the magic bottle and pulled it from her pocket.

The enchantress hissed softly as the jinni materialized. He bowed wordlessly, first to Jennifer and then to Norman, his gold jewelry jingling reassuringly.

"I have a question," Jennifer said. She glanced at Norman. She was going to give him an encouraging smile to say she knew what she was doing, but on second thought realized she didn't. "Could you carry me and Norman and Alexander to the other side of the forest wall and out of Malveenya's range of power?"

"Assuredly," the jinni answered.

"But Alexander would still be asleep," Malveenya pointed out hastily. "Unless, of course, that isn't important to you."

Of course it was. Despite everything, it still was. Jennifer tried a new approach. "You said you aren't allowed to harm anyone."

"That is correct."

"Directly?"

The jinni hesitated. "Directly?" he repeated.

"If I asked you for . . ." her mind groped, "well, say for twenty fine white horses. Could you give me that?"

The jinni was obviously confused, but he nodded.

"Sam, who sells horses back home, has only three or four very old mares. If I had twenty fine white horses to sell, that would drive Sam out of business."

"Ah!" the jinni said, his eyes sparkling.

"So actually my wish would harm Sam. Could you still grant it?"

"Sam would be harmed indirectly. I could grant your wish."

Jennifer nodded and pointed to a spot above Malveenya's head. "If I asked you to make that section of the ceiling fall this very second, could you?"

"Most swiftly."

Malveenya took a hurried step behind the table.

"If I asked you to make that table burst into flame, could you do that?"

The jinni nodded and Malveenya stepped closer to Alexander, where she felt Jennifer would be less likely to try something drastic. "Ah, little Miss Goody-Goody demonstrates her true character at last," she purred.

"What?" Jennifer said.

"Thought you were so good and pure of heart and better than me, didn't you? But see what happens when you get a little power."

"I'm just trying to protect myself," Jennifer objected.

Malveenya was smirking. "It always happens. Once you have the power to force people to do your will, there's no stopping you from using that power more and more." She was swirling her white dress in a seemingly absent manner to hide a little step in Jennifer's direction.

"That's not so!" Jennifer said. "If you just leave us alone, I won't use any power at all!"

"Careful," Norman warned. "Don't let her touch the bottle."

Malveenya ignored him and smiled at the girl in open disbelief.

"It's true!" Jennifer said. "I don't want to hurt anyone."

"Is that why you're threatening me?" Malveenya moved closer.

Jennifer darted a look at Norman. He obviously was assuming she had a plan and she didn't dare ask for his help with Malveenya so close. She took a step back and felt the wall behind her.

At that moment she knew that if she didn't make a wish right then—one that would stop Malveenya immediately—the enchantress would grab the magic bottle away and thereby increase her already vast powers. At the same moment, she also knew that even if the jinni could harm someone indirectly, she couldn't. She, and Norman, and Alexander were doomed.

Norman, suddenly realizing what was happening, called her name.

Malveenya saw the girl's mouth start to form a wish. She didn't know that it was a desperate wish, one meant to find a single strand of goodness in a hopeless situation. She only knew that there was no time to grab the bottle away and that she had to touch it quickly and—since there was no way to tell what Jennifer would ask for—that she must protect herself on all fronts.

"I wish to live forever!" Malveenya cried, while, at the exact same moment, Jennifer said, "I wish for the jinni's freedom from the bottle so he can do whatever he wants."

Instantly the jinni disappeared into a reddish cloud that somehow seemed to carry with it the smell of saltwater and the faint cry of sea gulls. Before anybody could be sure of this, however, he was gone.

There was another cloud in the room, but this one was glittering white and it floated exactly where Malveenya had been standing. With a soft sigh, it was sucked into the magic bottle, which grew warm in Jennifer's hand.

Out of the corner of her eye, she saw Kreech's form quiver as Malveenya's power disappeared. In the same instant that he regained his enormous wings, he sped out the open window. The next moment his wild scream of triumph reached them, but by then he was gone.

Magic

Numbly, Jennifer placed the magic bottle on the little shelf underneath the mirror. She saw without really noticing that the mirror's surface had become dull and clouded, as if it reflected a thick, empty fog. When Malveenya unintentionally traded places with the jinni, the mirror had become powerless.

Jennifer sighed and glanced around. "What now?" she asked.

Norman shook his head and knelt beside the sleeping prince. He was still breathing, but showed no signs of coming out of the spell.

"I don't know," the sorcerer whispered. "I don't know."

Jennifer ran her hand across Alexander's face and traced his lips with her fingertip. A tear ran down her cheek and fell onto Alexander's. If anything, the eyes seemed more tightly shut than she had remembered. She was thinking of Malveenya's words on sleeping forever. Norman knew the way out of the forest, but she couldn't just abandon poor, silly Alexander. She imagined the years to come: the forest slowly engulfing the house, vines pushing through the windows and under the doors, and she herself—white-haired and bent with age—dusting off an unchanged Alexander—forever young, forever handsome, but never able to laugh or smile again.

Jennifer tried to stop herself from thinking like this, but was unable to. Another tear fell on Alexander's face. The mouth, so warm and pink, almost seemed to move.

The answer was in her, but she couldn't find it.

Norman held her hand and tried to think of something to say.

Jennifer began sobbing even more. Her tear-filled eyes brimmed over—and the prince's nose seemed to twitch.

She threw herself across his chest, weeping uncontrollably. The prince gave a decided sneeze.

Jennifer immediately straightened.

Alexander's hand came up and rubbed his face. "Tickling," he muttered.

"What?" Jennifer said.

"Your hair is tickling me," the prince answered, rolling over and reaching for a blanket. When he couldn't find one, his eyes slowly opened and he looked at Jennifer.

"Yech!" he said, wiping his dampened face. "You've been crying all over me. And what happened to you? You look a mess!"

She started to apologize, but trailed off.

Alexander sat up. "Hey, what's been going on, anyway?" he said, trying to pull half-remembered events back together again. "The mirror. . . . I couldn't see. . . ." He stood up and rubbed his chest. "I feel like someone's been sitting on me," he muttered to himself. Then, seeing Norman for the first time, he said, "Who's the old geezer? And *what* have you done to my mirror?"

Norman stood up and patted Alexander on the shoulder. "So nice to finally meet you," he said. "Although I must say I liked you better asleep."

"I beg your pardon," Alexander said icily. "But do you have any idea to whom you are speaking? My father, the king—"

"Your father, the king, has an idiot for a son."

Before Alexander could protest, Norman gave a brief, but vivid, description of Jennifer's adventures with Malveenya.

"You did that for me?" Alexander asked her.

She nodded.

"But why?"

"I couldn't just leave you."

"No, that's true," Alexander agreed. He looked at her in silence for several seconds, then began pacing about the cottage.

Now Alexander may have had some faults, but he did know the rules of chivalry and he realized that he owed Jennifer his life. After only a brief delay, he cleared his throat. "Of course, we need to give you a suitable reward," he started. He cleared his throat again. "You're not married or engaged or anything?" He couldn't remember if she had ever mentioned this.

Jennifer shook her head.

"Would you like to marry me?" he asked.

"No. Thank you."

"My father, the king, will give us one of his castles on the . . ." The prince's voice died off and he scratched the back of his neck. He looked at her with a puzzled expression in his clear blue eyes. "Did I hear you say . . . ?" He hesitated because he was sure he had heard wrong and he didn't want to make himself look silly. "Did I hear you say, 'No'?"

"Yes, you did," Jennifer said.

Norman, sitting on the window seat, trying to make himself unobtrusive, dropped all pretense of not listening.

"It's very kind of you to offer," Jennifer told Alexander. "But it's unnecessary."

"Of course it's *unnecessary*," Alexander said, "but I'm still asking you."

"No." She was surprising herself, the words coming out before she knew what they would be. "You'll always be a very special friend, but I don't want to marry you."

Alexander shook his head in confusion. No one had ever said no to him before, but on the other hand, he didn't really want to marry Jennifer either; so he didn't know what to do. Deciding this needed thinking over, he went outside to sit on the chopping block, where he could be alone.

Jennifer looked at Norman, who shook his head also. "Good decision. He definitely makes a better impression when he's asleep."

Jennifer smiled. "No, it's not just that. In the last

couple of days I've learned some very important things about appearances."

Norman could feel himself beginning to panic, and he tried to think of a way to joke his way out of a serious conversation in which he was afraid he had too much to lose. But he couldn't come up with anything and merely stared silently at the floor.

"And," Jennifer continued somewhat shyly, "I guess I've seen that sometimes the people who seem to be the easiest to fall in love with aren't necessarily the best ones to be in love with."

Norman looked up slowly and couldn't remember why he had wanted to end the conversation. He smiled and Jennifer smiled back, and suddenly he found himself laughing.

This was the first time in years that he had done so, and now his entire body shook as he totally gave himself up to it. It started in his throat, but quickly spread to his chest and stomach, on down to the very tips of his fingers and toes until he thought he'd never be able to stop again. Each time he thought he'd gained control, it would bubble up again someplace else.

Jennifer, laughing too, until tears again streamed down her face, thought once more that that was why she was seeing things. "Strange how laughter makes someone look younger," she thought, noticing that there were fewer wrinkles in Norman's face.

But then she saw that his white beard was definitely fading away and that his hair was quickly becoming the bright, tangled red she had seen at their first meeting.

"Look, look," she cried, "the laughter's turning you young again!"

This news couldn't possibly have made him laugh any harder—only longer. And it was a good five minutes later before they were able to stand, exhausted and leaning against the walls, with only occasional mild giggles breaking loose.

Jennifer pushed her dark hair out of her eyes. "Oh, I love stories that end, 'And then everyone lived happily ever after,' " she said. But then she saw that someone was standing in the front door and the laughter died completely. "Hello, Old Witch," she said softly.

The old woman nodded, but kept staring at Norman. "The magic pool and I, we decided maybe I was a bit too nasty," she finally said. "I came to let you borrow the ring to change back, but I see you don't need it."

Norman shook his head.

Looking tired, the witch nodded. It had taken her all morning to reach the cottage and she saw that her trip was for nothing. Her yellow eyes noted the condition of the mirror and the absence of the prince. She sat wearily on the edge of the bed and looked from Norman to Jennifer, back to Norman. She sensed a change in their relationship, and was deep in thought for a few minutes.

"You're leaving, aren't you?" she said at last. "You won't be coming back and we won't even have a neighbor anymore."

Norman didn't answer because there was nothing to say.

"There's always been a sorcerer in the enchanted forest before," the Old Witch said. She sighed, scratched herself, then repeated it more softly.

Before either Norman or Jennifer could say anything, the back door flung open and Prince Alexander strode in.

He had finally made his decision, and what he had decided was that he was, after all, the king's only son, and what he asked for, he should get—whether he wanted it or not.

He explained this very carefully to Jennifer, who looked at him all the while with a faintly amused smile. "Are you listening to me?" he asked.

"No," she admitted.

Alexander turned to the old geezer for support and noticed, for the first time, that the old geezer had been replaced by someone about his own age. He blinked uncertainly at Norman, who only smiled innocently. Alexander glanced around the room helplessly, then took a quick step closer and whispered, "Who is that beautiful lady?"

"That," Norman said, his gray eyes twinkling brightly, "is the Old Witch."

Jennifer looked up and saw the Old Witch twirling the magic ring on her finger. Only she didn't look like the Old Witch anymore. For one thing, she was very young. Her straggly gray hair was now a thick, curly mane of silver. Her ragged black clothes had changed

into a flowing dark gown that shimmered with little points of color wherever the sun hit it. She gazed shyly down at her hands. And she was, indeed, beautiful.

Alexander looked at Norman as if he were crazy and walked across the room. He put on a brilliant smile. "Hi, there," he said. "My name is Alexander. My father is the king, you know."

"Hello," the Old Witch said in a husky whisper.

"What's your name?"

"Abitare," the Old Witch whispered. "It means, to live." Actually it had been so long since anyone had called her anything but Old Witch, she herself could no longer remember what her name was. But she thought Abitare had a nice sound to it, and she may have been right after all. She started to scratch, but caught herself at the last second and smoothed out a wrinkle in her dress instead.

"That's a very pretty name," Alexander said. "And you have the most beautiful golden eyes."

Norman didn't hear her answer because Jennifer was frantically nudging him.

"Do you think we should tell him?" she whispered.

"We could," Norman said. "Do you think he'd believe us?"

Jennifer smiled.

And then everyone *did* live happily ever after.